HIDDEN IN DARKNESS

DARKNESS II

NORA ASH

ABOUT THE AUTHOR

Nora Ash writes thrilling romance and sexy paranormal fantasy.

Visit her website to learn more about her upcoming books.

WWW.NORA-ASH.COM

CONNECT WITH NORA

Want to chat all things alpha? (and ruthlessly sexy book-boyfriends in general?)

Join Nora's Reader's Group:

EMAIL:
www.nora-ash.com/newsletter

ONE

There was a time I spent my days in front of my computer, writing about cultural issues and events in an effort to pay off my ever-increasing credit card debt. On occasion, mainly when I'd been a hermit for too long, I'd grab my laptop and venture to the nearest coffee shop. Sometimes I'd even smile at the other patrons over my caramel latte.

It had been four days since my life had changed, and I already missed the monotony. Some people were made out to be investigative reporters who lived life on the edge and got a kick out of flirting with danger. I was not one of those people.

Yet here I was, once again traipsing through the most crime-infested city in North America in search of clues that would pull me deeper into St. Anthony's seedy underbelly.

I pulled my coat tighter around myself in an attempt to hide from the other people hurrying along on the wet pavement. Not that any of them paid me any notice—they were all as eager as I was to get out of the rain. I told myself that my sense of foreboding was purely a result of knowing what would happen if the wrong people found out that I was still digging where I had explicitly been told not to—AKA the convoluted link between the mayor and the supes that I had inadvertently stumbled upon while blogging about my meeting with St. Anthony's favorite hero.

Lightning. I frowned at the thought of the superhuman who had been my unwitting access point to the darker part of the city. He might have saved me from a robbery at our first meeting, but he'd also pulled me into this mess. And he was the reason I'd met... *him.*

The Shade.

A shiver traveled down my spine at the memory of the man who had saved my life just last night, but demanded my submission in return. The Shade—the man rumored to have caused a thousand deaths and have a dark pit where his soul was meant to reside—had killed the men sent to torture me for information I didn't possess. He was no hero, yet he had been my only salvation from an untimely, and undoubtedly very unpleasant, death.

I could still feel the pleasurable tenderness deep inside from where he had joined his body with mine amid the broken bodies of my attackers, and I hated myself for the immediate clenching from down low at the thought of it.

I had never had sex like that, never even thought my body was capable of such excruciating pleasure—but it really shouldn't matter. The Shade was evil to the core, and I certainly shouldn't be getting all hot and flustered thinking about the most shameful thing I'd ever done.

Superhumans. Nothing but goddamn trouble.

And that was exactly why I was here now, on my way to digging myself deeper into the corruption in hopes that I would somehow be able to take control of my own life, and not depend on either *supe* to save me again. As much as I would have been screwed without The Shade's intervention last night, I didn't exactly have much faith in my continued survival if I relied on him or Lightning to get me out of this mess. They clearly had their own agendas, and being on either of them would likely get me into more trouble than any human being could handle.

The mark on the back of my neck, left by first Lightning and then The Shade, throbbed at my rebellious thoughts. I reached up to rub it, annoyed with the way the contact made my nipples tighten. There hadn't been any visual blemish on my skin from the last bite, but I could feel it buzz every time my thoughts drifted to either of the two men who had thought they could claim me.

Hopefully it would go away on its own soon.

My morose thoughts were interrupted when my gaze landed on the sign for Freeman Street. I turned right down it, keeping my eyes peeled for number 17. Thankfully, the area was well-lit, and I found the apartment building easily. Now all I needed to do was to convince my unsuspecting lead to talk to me.

I rang the buzzer to the address I'd found online and waited. The rain was coming down heavier now, and I huddled up in my coat and prayed Aaron would let me in before it soaked through to my clothes and skin.

"Yeah?" a male voice, scratchy with electronic disturbance, asked from the entry phone.

"Aaron Kempf?" I moved closer to the small box to make sure he could hear me over the noise from the street. "My name's Kathryn Smith. I was wondering if I could speak with you? It's about your friend, Peter."

A long silence followed.

"Hello?" I half-shouted after half a minute without a reply. "Can you hear me?"

No reply. I pressed the buzzer again, thinking the connection must have been cut.

"Oh, don't stand out in the rain, sweetheart. You'll get soaked to the bone."

I nearly jumped out of my skin at the friendly voice sounding from right behind me. I whipped around and came face to face with an old man wearing a hat and holding an umbrella. He smiled at me and pointed the keys in his hand toward the door. "Here, why don't I let us in so we can get out of this dreadful weather?"

I stepped out of his way with a grimace I hoped mimicked his smile, too astonished that anyone in this city trusted a stranger enough to just up and let them into their building like this to respond. Apparently, my drowned-mouse impression left me looking very non-threatening.

"Thank you," I managed as I slipped past him and into the stairway.

"Who are you here to visit?" the old man asked while we entered the small elevator. It was a tight squeeze fitting the two of us and his umbrella into it, but at least it seemed in a good enough state that I shouldn't worry about its capability of carrying more than one passenger. Not like the elevator that went up to my loft, which, frankly, seemed like a game of Russian roulette every time I got into it.

"Aaron Kempf." I pressed the button for the third floor. The old man pressed the button for the fourth, then clasped both hands around the handle of his umbrella, his bushy eyebrows raised.

"Is that right? I never thought him much of a ladies' man.

Always seemed fonder of the boys, if you know what I mean."

I cleared my throat uncomfortably and offered him a smile. "I'm just a friend."

"Hm. Well, if you fancy a cup of hot tea to warm up on after visiting your friend, my apartment is 4B."

My smile turned tight and I felt a blush threaten to creep up my neck. *Great.* It wasn't that I was unaccustomed to getting hit on by elder gentlemen—something about being a curvy girl seemed to draw them in, where their younger peers tended to completely overlook me. Maybe it was a left-over from times where food had to stretch for longer, and a chubby woman was easier to keep fed.

"Thanks, but I'm headed straight home after. Can't keep the boyfriend waiting." Yes, the "fake boyfriend" story. I was the only girl I knew of who frequently had to use that trick on pensioners. I shuffled closer to the wall and shot a desperate look at the display letting us know what floor we'd reached.

"What a pity," he said, offering me another smile. "Do come by if you change your mind." Then the elevator pinged, announcing that we'd reached the third floor, and I heaved an inaudible sigh of relief. It's not that I feared the old guy would force himself on me or anything—and if he did, I'd probably be able to outrun him even with my poor shape—but at age 26 I was still terrible at dealing with any sort of male interest. Probably because it was so scarce.

Perhaps I should just be thankful that this guy at least wasn't evil incarnate.

When the elevator door closed behind him I pulled my wandering thoughts together before they could once again stray to last night and all the things I really didn't need to think about right before an interview. I was somewhat successful, and when I finally knocked on Aaron's door, my focus was once again on the task at hand.

I could hear movement on the other side, and then the rattling of the chain before someone finally opened the door a few inches.

"What do you want?"

I frowned at his hostile tone. "Aaron? I just wanna talk. About Peter."

"I don't know anything about him. You need to leave." He started to close the door again, but I jammed my hand against it and stopped him.

"I know that's not true—I've seen the pictures of you two. Please, I really need to know what happened to him. I think... I think maybe the same thing is going to happen to me." Saying it out loud sent chills through me, but it got Aaron's attention. He stopped pushing against the door, and a moment later, he peeked out at me from behind the chain. His brown eyes were still narrowed, but as he took in my soaked and disheveled figure, they softened notably. Apparently, my appearance didn't scream "crazy serial killer."

"Can I come in, please?" I pressed, doing my best to look as nonthreatening as I possibly could. For a short, chubby woman who's just been soaked to the bone, that's pretty damn nonthreatening.

Aaron nodded and unhooked the chain so he could let me in.

I stepped into the small hallway and turned toward the young man I'd effectively stalked to get my answers. Hopefully, it would be worth it.

"Why do you think what happened to Peter is going to happen to you?" he asked as he guided me into a small, cluttered living room. "And what exactly is it you want from me?"

"I wrote an article about the mayor relying too much on the superhumans, and how corruption is spreading like wild-fire. Last night, someone attacked me." I clenched my hands, trying to keep my voice even. "Someone out there thinks I know something more than I do, and I need to figure out what is going on if I want a fighting chance at living through this. I know Peter disappeared after... after writing an article about something similar. I thought maybe it was connected?"

"And that I would know something?" Aaron shook his head, his lips pressed into a thin line. "Look, if the same people who went after Peter are after you, then I don't want to get involved. Peter wasn't the only one who disappeared—his two roommates, his sister and parents did, too."

I frowned. "I didn't see any mention of that when I researched it. You would think—"

"That six people disappearing would have made the news?" He slumped down on the rickety sofa and stared into the room. "I don't think you know who you're dealing with."

I felt like the wind had been knocked out of my lungs. Sure, being attacked by five armed men in an alley had put the amount of danger I was in into sobering perspective, but to exterminate Peter's entire family along with his room-mates? That was a level of evil I couldn't wrap my mind around.

"Look, I don't want to get dragged into this, okay? I was lucky they didn't know about... about Peter and me." Aaron's voice broke and he coughed, averting his gaze. "I was stupid to leave those pictures up, but it... it's so hard to pretend like he never existed."

"I'm sorry," I said softly. My heart went out to him—he

hadn't just lost a friend. For once, I was thankful for my loner status. My mom died several years ago, and I'd never known my father. It was a small consolation to know that my writing wouldn't hurt any loved ones.

"I won't mention you to anyone, I promise," I continued. "I just need to know if Peter told you anything about this that he didn't post? Any clues?"

He heaved a sigh and rubbed at his face. I was courteous enough to pretend I didn't see the wet shine in his eyes.

"If, by some miracle, you actually manage to take them down, will you make sure the world knows what they did to Peter?"

I nodded. If I survived this maelstrom of danger I'd unwittingly jumped into, then that was the least I could do. "I will."

"The mayor is behind a lot of the superhuman crime."

I heard the words, but it took me several moments before they sank in.

"I'm sorry, what do you mean 'behind'?" Sure, both Lightning and The Shade had hinted that the mayor was corrupt, but I'd pictured something along the lines of being dodgy with the tax budget. Not... whatever this was.

"I mean that, according to Peter, he's either working for the bad superhumans, or they are working for him. He said he needed proof of which way around it was, but he was certain that what he wrote in his article was only the tip of the iceberg. He was trying to figure out how to break into the mayor's house to go through his files when he... disappeared. If you really want to do this, you should look for a file labeled 'Blue Jay' or 'Blue Sparrow,' or something like that. And anything related to Bright. He seemed to believe there was a connection between Bright and the mayor."

I frowned, resisting the urge to pull out my notepad and a pen. If this was a credible lead, I was pretty certain I didn't want any written proof of my knowledge of it. "And what's in that file?"

Aaron shrugged. "I don't know. But that's what Peter said he needed to prove that the mayor is behind all the bad shit in this city."

TWO

I had to resist the urge to call Trish on the way home and let her know what I'd uncovered. If everyone the mayor thought knew anything about what Peter had discovered was now dead, I didn't want to bring her into it until I had something solid. That way, we would both have her newspaper's protection and I wouldn't cause my best friend's death.

Which meant that I had to sort through this new information on my own.

When I finally made it home, my brain felt heavy from spending the entire way from Aaron's apartment thinking over what he'd said, and what I was pretty sure would be the onset of a cold if I didn't get out of my wet, cold clothes.

I had just changed into my white-with-pink-piglets footie pajamas and poured myself a steaming cup of coffee, preparing for a night in front of the computer trying to figure out my next move, when the sensation of being watched made every hair on the back of my neck stand on end.

Oh, God, no. Please, no.

In the three seconds it took for me to accept that

someone was there, my mind whirled with every single crime scene photo I'd ever seen on the news or Internet. Previously, I might have spent time trying to convince myself that my instincts screaming at me that someone was in the apartment were wrong, but I'd had too much recent experience with dangers lurking in the shadows to ignore them.

I grabbed a knife off the block on the kitchen counter and spun around, weapon raised.

A large, black-clad figure stared at me from the other end of the kitchen

The Shade.

The Shade was in my home.

My mind switched gears instantly, the images in my head turning into memories of my last encounter with him. The dirty brick wall, his slanted smirk, the feel of his hands on my hips and his cock inside of me.

My involuntary whimper made heat rush to my face. I tightened my grip on the knife with both hands, pointing it at him. "What do you want?

His white teeth gleamed. "Really, kitten?"

"Really *what?*" I spat. I hated that he was making me feel embarrassed. I shouldn't have felt anything but terror at having The Shade appear in my kitchen.

"A bread knife?" He tutted and then turned, walking further into my studio apartment. "We really need to teach you some self-defense."

"What do you want?" I repeated. His dismissal only amplified my anger, which thankfully went a long way to calming my initial burst of fear and adrenaline.

"Is that a way to greet guests?" The Shade taunted. He didn't even look over his shoulder at me, instead opting to explore my home. I warily followed, keeping an eye on him while making sure there was plenty of distance between us, the knife still clutched in my hand.

"I don't usually draw out the welcome mat for burglars."

The Shade chuckled and finally turned around to face me again. He rested a hip against the back of my sofa, looking seriously out of place in his dark suit and with the two sword handles sticking up over his shoulders. "Drop the knife. The only one you're going to hurt with that thing is yourself."

I stubbornly maintained my grip on it. "What. Do. You. Want?"

Without warning, the air around The Shade erupted into a dark burst, and when I blinked to clear my eyes, he was standing right in front of me, his imposing body taking up way too much of my personal space. His blue eyes were heated as he grasped my chin and wrapped the other arm around my waist.

"I find it very endearing when you try to boss me around."

I swallowed thickly, finding it hard to breathe with his hands on me, even though the soft leather covering his fingers kept my skin from sparking at his touch. With the fire in his eyes and the purring huskiness of his deep voice, it was impossible not to remember the intimate details of our previous encounter. My heart pounded, and when his gaze dipped to my lips, my tongue flicked out to moisten them on its own. *Oh, God.* Why did this man have so much control over my body?

The Shade made a sound deep in his throat that resembled a mix between a growl and a groan. "Just the scent of you has me ready to fuck."

His crudeness made my brain snap back to reality just in

time for me to realize what the hardness pressing against my stomach was.

No. No, I couldn't give in again.

Panic, despite the pang of longing between my thighs, made me fumble and drop the knife with a clatter on the floor, nicking my index finger on its way down. I cursed and pressed my uninjured hand against The Shade's chest, leaning away from his smoldering gaze.

"Don't!"

His decadent mouth pursed, and I was sure he was arching an eyebrow at me underneath his mask. "Don't what? Fuck you?"

"Y-yes." A blush heated my cheeks. Hearing it said back to me made me realize how ridiculous the request was. He was The Shade. Rape was probably an everyday pastime for him. Yet even as I thought it, something in the back of my mind protested wildly at the idea of the man who had claimed and saved me forcing himself on me. Undoubtedly the same idiotic something that felt inexplicably safe wrapped in the villain's arms.

His leather-clad finger touched my chin in a light caress, letting the tip brush over my bottom lip. I shivered involuntarily in response.

"As much as I would love to remind you exactly how much you enjoy it when I fuck you, that's not what I'm here for, kitten."

"Then why are you here?" To my chagrin, it sounded a lot breathier than I'd intended, and I was painfully aware of the sweet throbbing down low.

"I wanted to remind you that, when I told you not to do any reporter snooping without my explicit permission, I meant it."

My eyes widened, and I had to bite my cheek to stifle a gasp. *How could he possible know...?* I had taken every precaution to ensure I wasn't followed when I went to visit Aaron.

"I haven't done any *snooping*," I lied, trying to channel my most trustworthy facial expression. "Honest. I was just out for some coffee."

The Shade snorted, and something other than heat glowed in his supernatural eyes. "I don't recommend lying to me again, Kathryn. It's not gonna end well."

I gaped up at him, the odd comfort of being locked in his embrace waning. As much as my body reacted to his presence, my brain was still all too aware of the threat his bulky mass presented.

"Let's try this without you testing my patience, shall we?" he asked, bringing his thumb up so my chin was caught in his grasp. His hold was still gentle, but there was enough firmness to make me rethink pulling away. "What were you doing tonight?"

As much as I didn't want to tell The Shade I'd gone against his command—and especially not say anything that would put poor Aaron on his radar—I also had no desire to test the limits of his patience.

"I followed a lead." I jutted out my chin in defiance when his eyes narrowed ever so slightly.

"And my order of not doing exactly that?" His voice was laced with false sweetness. It only fueled my own frustration.

"Look, I'm not about to sit back and pretend like I'm not in serious trouble here," I said, finally pulling my chin out of his grasp. "I'm clearly a target, so waiting around for them to strike again is not an option."

"So you thought disobeying me was the safer choice?" His eyes flashed dangerously, the saccharine gone from his deep voice. "I told you I would protect you—blindly following whatever leads you think you find makes that very hard. When I give you an order, I expect you to follow it. Got it?"

I frowned. "Why do you care if I'm safe or not?"

Annoyance filtered across his expression, and it dawned on me that he was most definitely not used to being questioned. "You're *mine*. I protect what's mine. Do I need to remind you?"

I gasped when he let his fingertips dance over the back of my neck, and the place where he'd bitten me flared with a tingling sensation that made me moan and my nipples pebble. *Oh, God!* That felt *way* too good—not at all like the subtle pulsing I'd gotten used to.

When he eased the pressure and my haze of lust cleared, I glared at him. "That's so not cool."

His lips parted in a grin. "You're the first human I've met who's brave enough to give me this much attitude. I like it."

Brave... stupid. It was a blurry line. But I wasn't entirely sure I wanted The Shade's appreciation—even if the mutinous part of me felt an exhilarated rush. It was probably related to the damn mark on my neck. In either case, it needed to be thoroughly ignored.

"So, are you just here to check up on me?" I asked, trying to get The Shade's attention far away from the mark he'd left on me and what he could do with it.

"Yes. And it seems it was warranted. I need the name and address of whoever you visited."

I hesitated. "I... I can't give you that." He narrowed his eyes at my refusal, and I hastily continued. "I promised my

source he wouldn't get dragged into this, and no offense but...
if I give *you* his details, my word is worth nothing. And I
realize you don't care about that, but I really do and... and
you'd have to force it out of me!"

Granted, the last bit was not the smartest thing to say to a
man with The Shade's reputation, and I winced the second it
slipped past my lips.

To my surprise, the big brute snorted.

"Such a feisty little human. You do understand that I
could force it out of you with very little effort?"

I swallowed nervously and nodded. "A-are you
going to?"

He smirked. "Maybe later. I find the idea of you tied up
and fighting my will... stimulating. But tonight, I don't have
that kind of time, so either you volunteer the information, or
I will track down the guy myself after I've gone about my
business. And trust me, kitten—it will be *much* more
unpleasant for him if I have to do the legwork."

I had a moment's worth of wondering why he didn't just
use some of his superpowers on me—or inflicted enough pain
on me to make me cave—but then I realized that his current
strategy was much more efficient. I had no doubt he would
hurt Aaron to prove a point if I didn't comply—and I
couldn't let that happen.

"*Okay!* Just... promise me you won't hurt him. He's not a
part of this. You won't gain anything from killing him."

The Shade pursed his lips. "That entirely depends on
how harmless he really is. You have no way of knowing if
he's an informant. I do. But if he is truly no one, then he
won't ever know I was there. Now—the name, Kathryn. And
his address."

"Aaron Kempf," I muttered. "17 Freeman Street, Apartment 3B."

"Good girl." The Shade teased a finger over my bottom lip again and then released my waist, stepping back. "And what did this Aaron Kempf tell you?"

I drew in a relieved breath. "That his friend, who was looking into the connection between the mayor and Bright, was wiped off the face of the Earth, along with his family and roommates. And that this friend knew the mayor was behind a lot of superhuman crime. He was looking for proof when he disappeared."

"And he used that exact word? 'Behind'?"

"Well, he wasn't sure if he was working for them, or they were working for him, but yes. Do you know anything about this? Or about how Bright might be involved?"

To my utter surprise, he actually answered my question.

"Bright is one of our leaders," he said, shifting his gaze from me to the windows lining my apartment's outer wall. "A relatively new one, but powerful. Resourceful. And very tricky. As for the mayor... Well, I'll be looking into that."

"Wait, so... one of your leaders is openly a *villain*? How in the world does he get away with that?"

The corner of The Shade's mouth curved up a little at my outrage. "Heroes and villains... such human conceptions. Our hierarchy is built on strength and cunning, not morals. Some use human weakness as an argument that you should be protected, but really, it's just an excuse to look after their own interests. Yet you hail them as heroes."

I frowned. "What possible scheming could there be behind a superhuman saving sick children from that hospital fire last month?" Or me from a robbery. Granted, I'd written about the dangers of giving the supes too much free reign over the city, but even I couldn't argue that, without super-humans, a lot of people would undoubtedly be dead. Myself included.

"Ah, Wildflower, the gentle soul who went into a burning building to save so many lives out of the kindness of her heart," The Shade sneered. "And was awarded a handsome fee for her generous spirit. If only she could have saved all the children. She set that fire herself, you know. Most likely to kill the kid who survived that high-profile home invasion in July. You remember the one—too traumatized to speak, but kept drawing pictures of masked men and women? He was in that hospital, and he never made it out."

My jaw dropped in horror. "You're not serious!"

"Oh, but I am. Good, evil... it's all just different shades of gray. Sure, some supes actually have a bit of a soft spot for humans, but there's always an angle. Some just play heroes to ensure you don't start trying to hunt us down and eradicate us in earnest. As long as you think some of us live to protect you, you remain complacent. And we all prosper."

"But you are so much stronger than us!" I protested, still trying to wrap my mind around the less than pretty picture he was painting. "Surely, you don't need deception to get what you want."

"There are far, far more humans than there are supes. If it came to all out war, you would win. So, we stay in the shadows."

Well, at least that was something. I wrapped my arms around myself. "And you? What's your angle? Why do you insist on *protecting* me?"

The Shade turned his gaze back on me, and before I managed to still my heart's uneasy flutter, both his thick arms were wrapped around me, pulling me tight against his body.

I gasped. It wasn't often I felt delicate and feminine, what with my sturdy figure, but in The Shade's strong embrace it was impossible not to—he was just so *big,* oozing masculinity from every pore. Even my ugly footie pajamas and rain-squashed hair didn't make me feel any less like a fragile little thing in need of his protection.

I flushed at my errant thoughts and desperately tried to focus on the scary aspect of being in the dangerous supe's arms. The heated stare he was leveling at me from his superior height didn't exactly help things.

"I find the thought of your death unpleasant," he said, his voice low and husky. "That is why I protect you. How can I feel your tight little pussy milk my cock again if some idiotic human kills you while I am preoccupied elsewhere?"

I sputtered at the deadpan answer, but my body seemed to appreciate his candidness. A strong surge of arousal made my abdomen pulse.

When he bent his head and let his lips brush over mine, I parted them without resistance.

He growled, the rich sound making moisture seep between my thighs and my heartbeat quicken. Then his tongue flickered in between my lips, and a groan slipped out of my own throat in response. Delicious heat overwhelmed my senses along with the dark, musky taste of him and the feel of his tongue caressing mine. My knees gave way, but he caught me easily.

At that moment, there was only him and me, only the desire thrumming through my body and the feel of the man it longed for holding and caressing me. It didn't matter who he was, it didn't matter that everyone called him evil. He was everything I needed, and in his arms I felt safe. *Home.*

The blissful insanity lasted until he pulled away from the kiss.

I blinked up at him, still open-mouthed. My lips felt swollen, and I could sense an impressive blush spread from my chest up to my cheeks. What was it with this man? How did his touch keep making me ignore all the horrors I knew about him?

"I have to go." The Shade let one of his hands stroke across my cheek before he stepped back, slowly melting into the shadows. "The next time you see me, we will finish this. I promise."

THREE

Clearly, I was a depraved slut. The only thing that had stopped this trait from developing sooner was probably just the lack of sexy men crawling through my kitchen window before now.

When I climbed out of bed the morning after The Shade's visit, I pointedly refused to look at the vibrator I'd tossed on the bed in exhaustion during the night. Shortly after his departure I'd given in to the insistent throbbing between my legs and allowed the vivid memories of his—and at a particularly low point—Lightning's hands and bodies wrapped around mine. The result was much like the moral hangover I'd woken up with during my college years after my first encounter with tequila. I felt dirty and ashamed, and even a long shower didn't do much to alleviate my guilt.

But really, what was a girl to do? Questionable morals aside, both men were beyond sexy, bordering on godly in their overwhelming masculinity, and the way I'd felt in The Shade's arms last night....

Not to mention the sex. Oh, my Lord, the *sex*.

Before The Shade had swept out of the darkness to save me, I hadn't truly known what sex was. Sure, I'd slept with a couple of men over the years, but no one had ever made me feel so completely in lust, and certainly no one had ever filled me so thoroughly, taken me so completely.

It was really not that odd, from an objective point of view, that my ovaries flipped out at the mere thought of the powerful males who had claimed me as theirs. And what was I meant to do—tell The Shade no?

I snorted at that impossible idea while I wrapped my hair in a towel and pulled on a bathrobe, trying to forget how my body had begged for everything he did in that alley. And how he had never forced me. It was so freaking impossible to align everything I thought I'd known about the monster we called The Shade with the man who made my blood sing. As for Lightning... I didn't even know how to start processing his half-claim, nor did I know how he would react to The Shade's mark. If I ever saw him again, of course.

One thing was certain—if either of them planned on returning, I somehow needed to ensure that they explained exactly what their expectations were. They had both called me *theirs,* and I was starting to catch on to the idea that it wasn't just an empty phrase. At least not for The Shade.

A delicate shiver traveled down my spine at the memory of his husky promise to return and finish "this." After the heated kiss we'd shared, I had a pretty good feeling of what "this" was. Maybe swinging by my doctor to talk about birth control wouldn't be the worst idea, since I didn't fancy taking another morning-after pill the next time The Shade decided to stop by.

I frowned, fiddling with my fluffy bath robe. *Birth control.* It seemed like such concerns should belong to a new relationship, not... whatever the heck this was, but I somehow doubted The Shade would be open to the concept of condoms. If they even came in his size. *Christ.*

I'd just decided to make an appointment with my doctor that same morning when the sound of my letterbox made me jump.

It was several hours too early for it to have been the mailman, and my heart pounded unevenly as I began to imagine all sorts of unpleasant scenarios. For a moment I wished I had some way of contacting The Shade, but quickly pushed that unwelcome thought away. Even if my ovaries didn't care about who he was, I wasn't about to let myself believe I could truly count on him to keep me safe. No, I had to rely on myself, and to the extent that it didn't risk her life, Trish.

I crept closer to my front door, prepared for the worst. But instead of a small bomb or conspicuous-looking powder, I only found a white envelope made from expensive-looking paper on the floor. My name was handwritten on it in sweeping, inky letters, but there was no address underneath it. Clearly, it'd been hand delivered.

I picked it up and let my fingers run over the thick paper. Only when I flipped it over did I notice the city's emblem in the form of a wax seal, and my heart sped up again. It came from the mayor's office.

FOUR

Dear Ms. Kathryn Smith, author of "The Dark City":

The Honorable Chris Wilkins, mayor of St. Anthony, requests your presence at the annual Autumn Ball on Thursday, the 21st of September at the Wisenger-Randham building, 253 23rd St.

Please bring this invitation and the enclosed press badge to show at the door upon arrival.

Yours Sincerely,

Ruth Portland
    Press Secretary
    Mayor's office

My heart thumped hard behind my ribs as my brain tried to frantically work out why in the world the mayor would invite *me,* of all people. Most likely, he was the man behind my attempted kidnapping and torture, and I couldn't think of a single, pleasant reason for him to invite me to the ball of the year. And, in the unlikely case that he *wasn't* behind my very bad night, why would he invite *me?* I was no one.

I picked up the laminated press badge that came along with the letter, intent on staring at it until I could think up a helpful answer. Preferably one that didn't include my painful demise. A small, folded up note was attached to the backside of the clip.

Frowning, I pulled it out and unfolded it. On cheap, blue-lined notepaper, someone had scribbled:

Bat your eyelashes, kitten, and ask him who caters the ball and how old the chandeliers are.

If he believes you're dumb enough to be of no threat, he won't waste resources going after you again.

IT WAS UNSIGNED, but that particular pet name made it plenty obvious who the author was.

Evidently, The Shade had found a way to get me off the mayor's radar.

I could only hope his plan was well thought through,

because if it wasn't, I would literally be handing myself over to the man who wanted me dead.

But I really didn't have much of a choice. If I didn't go, not only would I have to deal with The Shade's wrath—I'd also pass up my possibly only chance at placating the mayor.

And... a thought occurred to me while I was nervously playing with the edges of the press badge. If I had an invitation, I could enter the mayor's mansion, and possibly go searching for the evidence poor Peter had been after, before he was killed.

In fact, it would be downright stupid of me not to.

Yes, I needed to go to this ball, make the mayor believe I was nothing but a dimwitted blogger, and then find a way to snoop through his things.

The only thing left for me to do was to pray that my dark protector was as good of a manipulator as his reputation would suggest. And buy a nice dress, of course.

WHEN I CLIMBED out of the taxi and looked up at the impressive estate that framed the mayor's prestigious ball, it wasn't just the knowledge that I was quite probably stepping into the lion's den that had my palms sweaty. All of the city's elite were there, parading in front of the flashing cameras in their finery, and I felt sorely out of place.

I'd managed to find a blue chiffon dress that, even though it clung a little too tightly to my rounded features, made me feel pretty when I looked in the mirror. But it wasn't anywhere near the same league as the flashy pieces of couture hanging off the tall, slender women on powerful men's arms as they walked down the red carpet rolled out for the guests.

It took all my willpower to not hunch my shoulders and try to hide as I climbed the stairs to the mayor's mansion, clutching the press badge around my neck like a shield.

"Name?"

I jumped and looked up at the burly guard with a clipboard and an earpiece who blocked the door. He was eying my press badge, and then scrutinizing my face, probably wondering why he hadn't seen me at any of these events before.

"Kathryn Smith," I managed without a stammer, even as my stomach did an unpleasant flip-flop. If the Shade had miscalculated, then there was every chance I'd get hauled into a private room and beaten to death for the sheer audacity of showing up on the mayor's doorstep.

But the guard simply scanned his clipboard and then nodded. "Go on in, Miss Smith, and enjoy your evening."

"Thanks," I croaked, and then I stepped through the doors to the lion's den.

As it turned out, the lion's den was pretty darn swank.

Even though the mansion was fairly modern, the inside of the house had been made up in old European nobility style. I made my way through thickly carpeted hallways lined with expensive paintings and sculptures, wondering where the mayor got all this wealth from while the city was struggling underneath him. I also made a mental note not to ask him that, if I got the chance for an interview. Blonde, airhead bloggers did not ask about financial strains—they complimented the beautiful interior, just like The Shade had instructed.

When I finally stepped into the ballroom, the glamour

nearly made me step right back out. Chandeliers glowed from the high ceilings with their thousands of beautiful crystals, the panelings and floors were rich mahogany, and in the vast space the entirety of St. Anthony's dressed-up elite milled around, chatting and dancing to the live string quartet. Everyone from TV stars to athletes to business moguls and politicians, and—

Blue, glowing eyes met mine just as I realized who the charcoal-and-crimson, skintight suit my gaze had been drawn to belonged to.

The masked hero lit up in a bright, teasing grin, while dread flopped down heavily in my stomach. *Oh, God.*

"Kittykat!"

Lightning.

My face tightened into a tense smile when the hero broke away from the small cluster of people, heading straight toward me. I hadn't expected him, or any other superheroes, to be present at this event, and I really, really didn't want to face this particular superhuman while trying to impersonate a semi-decent spy.

"Well, well, Little Miss Reporter," Lightning said once he stopped in front of me. Despite the teasing smile, there was sharpness behind his blue gaze, and I realized that he was not at all pleased to see me there. Possibly because he'd told me to keep my nose out of this. He nevertheless managed to give my cleavage a good leer.

"You clean up well. Here on official blogging duty?"

"Yes." I held up my press badge and craned my neck so I could look him in the eye. "I couldn't say no to an opportunity to experience the famous Autumn Ball as an insider. Everything here is just so amazing! Like, how old are these chandeliers?"

Lightning narrowed his eyes a touch at my chirpy tone, but he didn't call me out, either. Instead, his smile turned brighter, and before I knew it he'd wrapped his arm around my shoulders. "Well, I don't know, kittykat, but why don't we go ask the mayor? I'm sure he'd be happy to answer any questions you have about the ball."

Short of beating at him to be left alone, I had no choice but to allow Lightning to drag me   across the crowded floor to the small group he'd left.

"Kathryn, meet our honorable host, Mayor Wilkins, and Elias Shaw, CEO of Shaw Industries. Gentlemen, this is Kathryn Smith, a journalist I bumped into a few nights ago. I'm sure she would love the chance to ask a few questions."

I felt the blood drain from my face when I stared up at the man who had likely ordered my kidnapping and torture.

I'd practiced what I'd say to him in front of the mirror until I'd perfected the bubble-headed tone, but I'd planned on choosing the how and when. Getting dragged practically by the scruff of my neck like a sacrificial lamb was not a part of the plan.

The mayor was exactly as tall and imposing as he seemed on TV, and his trademark, somewhat aggressive smile was plastered across his sharp features. His cold, gray eyes bore into mine, nailing me to the spot.

"It's such an honor, sir," I managed. I felt a smile of my own, as fake as the mayor's, stretch my cheeks. "Your house is very beautiful. I'm dying to know, how old are these amazing chandeliers?"

The mayor's gaze momentarily followed my finger toward the ceiling before returning to me. "They're French 18th century. Miss Kathryn Smith... aren't you the young reporter who wrote quite the scathing piece on our hero here?"

Right to the point, then. I did my best not to swallow nervously under his scrutinizing look. There was no warmth behind those cool eyes. But before I managed to produce a reply, Lightning intervened.

His hand slid from my shoulder down to my butt, giving it a firm pinch. "Oh, that's water under the bridge, Wilkins. The girl was just a bit insulted that I didn't stick around after the interview. I made up for it later that night."

Thankfully, I could disguise my outrage at his insinuation behind my instant blush, and I even managed a strangled noise that could be taken for a coy giggle. It seemed to do the trick, because the mayor's piercing eyes finally moved from me to the hero, his posture relaxing just a fraction of a hair. He'd recognized my name, all right, and I was pretty sure it wasn't just from reaming out Lightning. I suppressed a shudder at the uninvited memories of being chased through dark alleyways like an animal and pressed closer to Lightning, suddenly happy he was there. His morals might have been somewhat questionable, but he was also the closest thing I had to protection in this wasp's nest.

"I didn't mean for it to come across as harsh as it did," I said, smiling until my cheeks hurt. "I'm just thankful Lightning was kind enough to forgive me."

Lightning made a rude snicker next to me, and my blush deepened at the obvious insinuation. He was so... unbelievably crude! But at least it was working. The mayor shared a slanted grin with the superhuman and then returned his attention to Elias Shaw, continuing a conversation about the stock market that Lightning had obviously interrupted by dragging me into their midst.

I breathed a silent sigh of relief and glanced up at Lightning to show my appreciation, despite his less than savory way of going about this whole protector role he'd adopted.

The hero spared me a short look, his eyes conveying a silent warning before he returned his attention to the two powerful men. He didn't have to spell it out—if I wanted to keep under the radar, I needed to continue playing the part.

I pulled my phone out of the matching clutch I'd bought with the dress and cleared my throat, interrupting the mayor and Elias Shaw. "Excuse me, sir, would it be possible to hear your thoughts about the ball?"

The mayor turned to me once more, but this time, his expression resembled nothing but polite indifference. "Certainly, Miss Smith. Ask away."

I began rambling off mundane questions about the decorations, the guest list, and the origin of his yearly ball, all the while smiling brightly and feigning intrigue at the mayor's equally mundane answers. It didn't take long for him to make his excuses, leaving me behind with the superhuman and the CEO.

"Nicely done, Kittykat," Lightning said as I turned off the audio recording app on my phone. "I can never get a moment without Wilkins stuck to my side at these events. Who knew boring the man to death was the answer?"

Elias made a rude sound. "Please, as if you'd willingly give up the glorious photo ops of you two bonding over '*the greater good of the city.*' You're as stuck to him as he is to you, my friend."

Lightning laughed, his eyes twinkling, and I realized the two men were at the very least on friendly terms. Up until then I'd been too preoccupied to really pay attention to the

CEO, but the idea that he and Lightning had some sort of bond sparked my curiosity.

I turned toward him, still with the cheek-torturing smile plastered on my face—and nearly choked on my own tongue.

"Well, some of us don't have literally billions to lean on. I rely on my charms to further the city's well-being, while you play Monopoly. We both end up smiling for the cameras, shaking Wilkins' hand."

Lightning's dry tone made Elias smirk in an all-too-familiar gesture, but it wasn't the way his perfect mouth slanted with amusement that made my mouth dry and my heart pound with recognition. It was... everything about him.

He was big—so very big, though the sleek business suit and tie did much to conceal what was obviously a heavily muscled body. His face was perfect in its masculinity, crowned by a shaved head, and I had a faint memory of seeing him in a few news clippings. *Elias Shaw.* I had vague knowledge about Shaw industries, but only to the extent of knowing that it was one of the biggest players in town. But that was not why my breathing had turned shallow and my ovaries spasmed. It wasn't memories of pictures that had my body reeling.

My eyes swept to his, but no eerie blue shine met my gaze. His eyes were a dark gray, though unlike the mayor's, there was a smoldering heat behind them. He wasn't a superhuman.

And it wasn't *him.*

Maybe it was just his size and the squareness of his jaw, and that perfectly sculptured mouth that threw my body off in a big way. I drew in a deep breath, trying to calm myself down. Unfortunately, Elias picked that moment to turn his head, catching my flustered gaze.

A small smile grazed his lips, and I realized he must have thought I was ogling him. Which I suppose I kind of was. My face heated up further, and I quickly shifted my gaze to Lightning, feigning ignorance.

"Why *do* you come to these events? I wouldn't think you needed to lobby for any cause."

The hero scoffed, his hand slipping down to catch mine so he could bring it to his lips. "We must all put on a good front, Little Miss Reporter. And yours is slipping. You really should ask me about my workout routine—or what color eyes I prefer in women."

My skin tingled where he had kissed it, and I did my best to ignore my already-flustered body's heated response. No matter how much of an ass he was being, I couldn't deny that I still found him attractive. Of course, judging by my reaction to Elias just a moment ago, I was apparently turning into some hormonal time bomb. It was disturbing.

"Green."

"Hm?" I looked up from my hand to Lightning, whose teasing gaze had gained just a sliver of heat. "I prefer green eyes, with just a hint of blue. They make me think of standing in an endless forest, peeking up at the sky through thousands of leaves."

For a moment I thought he was still trying to help me keep my cover as a dimwit. Then I realized he'd—albeit somewhat poetically— picked my eye color.

"That's lovely, Lightning, but maybe you want to save some of that fabled charm for the other journalists? It's a long night, after all."

Elias' dry voice ripped me out of my quiet meltdown. I snagged my hand back, leveling a glare at the hero for messing with my head like that, after how he had manipulated my will the last time we saw each other. He only gave me a wink in return, then turned his attention back to Elias.

"Ah, but do the other journalists blush as prettily? I think not."

I had to fight back the urge to slap the smirk off his face. As much as I needed to play the part of an airhead, I was still inwardly seething after only half an hour of this charade. The fact that Lightning seemed to get a kick out of it made my palms itch to give him a good whack.

"Maybe not, but they seem to be awaiting your arrival nonetheless."

Both Lightning and I looked in the direction Elias nodded. A clump of serious-looking reporters had surrounded mayor Wilkins and were now eyeballing the hero.

Lightning sighed. "Seems it's time for that photo. I shall return later. Elias. Miss Smith."

I watched Lightning's retreating back, definitely not staring at his perfectly defined butt flexing with each step. It was near impossible for me to get a good read on that man. It *seemed* like he had been trying to help me keep my cover, but he also seemed perfectly fine with leaving me to my own devices.

Perhaps he was more of a "protection within reason" sort of hero, rather than the full-time nanny type. Or maybe he had some ulterior motive? The fact that he was playing nice with the mayor like this, while calling him corrupt behind his back, certainly suggested as much.

"Would you care for a dance?"

The unexpected question jolted me out of my contemplations, and I turned around to look at Elias, who was holding out an oversized hand toward me.

"Oh, uh..." During all my fretting, somehow the possibility of this situation had completely escaped my mind. No one ever asked me to dance.

"I... I'm a terrible dancer. I'd just step on your toes."

His perfect mouth quirked into one of those inexplicably familiar smirks. "I'm a strong lead."

I would have continued my protests, mainly because I had never danced without consuming a hefty dose of alcohol first—and never the kind of slow, elegant ballroom dancing expected at the mayor's ball—but Elias grabbed my hand and pulled me toward him, leaving me no choice.

As he led me to the dance floor, my hand securely wrapped in his, I had another sense of déjà vu. Perhaps having unlimited funds behind your name gave a man the same self-confidence as having superpowers. The level of inherent dominance certainly had the same effect on my pathetic ovaries, and I had to bite the inside of my cheek to stop my thoughts from turning decidedly unsavory. Apparently, my body wasn't going to ignore Elias' resemblance to the man who had claimed it so thoroughly.

Elias put one hand on my waist and positioned me against him as if I was as light and lithe as a ballerina, and my body easily shifted into position in front of him. *Huh.*

I'd never been a graceful dancer, but with this mountain of a man, moving freely felt easy. Only when I saw his responding smile, warm and completely free from any sarcasm or innuendos, did I notice my own lips were stretched into a grin. For that moment I wasn't a scared or insecure girl, nor a reporter trying to get to the bottom of a story. I was just a woman in the arms of a sexy man, sharing a dance and a smile. It felt amazing.

"You're a blogger?"

"Yeah. Mainly about culture and that sort of thing."

"What made you choose that profession?"

There was no judgment in his voice, just curiosity. The way his eyes scanned my face made me feel like he was genuinely interested—which was puzzling. I couldn't wrap my mind around why a smoking-hot billionaire would have any interest in me, a chubby girl from at least five steps down the social ladder. The warmth of his closeness made me decide not to care, at least for this one dance.

"It's a lot of freedom. I like to write, which is why I studied journalism in college. I set my own hours and can choose the articles I want to write."

"So you value freedom more than the security of a nine-to-five."

I wasn't sure if it was a question or a statement, but I nodded nonetheless.

"And what about you? What made you decide to be a business entrepreneur, Mr. Shaw?"

His smile slanted. "Money. I like money."

"And power?" The question just slipped out and I bit my lip, searching his face for any offense taken. There was none.

"Yes, and power. It's a different kind of freedom than what your blogging gives you, but power and money do provide certain liberties."

I don't know what I'd expected from a big-shot CEO during a slow dance, but it wasn't honesty. I told him as much.

Elias shrugged, never loosening his grip on me. "There are so many masks and hidden agendas in this city. Sometimes, I just want a beautiful woman to see a real part of me."

I flushed at the compliment and looked down to hide my embarrassment. Despite Lightning's crude comments about my *curves* and The Shade's obvious interest in getting naked and sweaty with me, I wasn't used to being called beautiful or have a man—at least under the age of sixty—pay this kind of attention to me.

Then his words struck another chord, and I frowned and looked back up at him.

His gray eyes made my blood warm. *Masks.* Had he not reminded me so much of the masked villain, I would not have thought there could be a double meaning to that one word, but...

The music changed and we stopped dancing.

Elias lifted his hand from mine and touched it gently to my cheek, and the warmth in my veins concentrated just south of my navel in a hot spike of desire.

"Thank you for the dance."

Only two men had ever been able to affect me like that, and one of them was currently across the room, talking to the press. I suppressed a soft moan when Elias' stroked his fingers from my cheek to my bottom lip, caressing it gently and far more intimately than he had any business doing.

That was when I saw it. The thin scar stretching across his lip when his mouth curved in a smile as intimate as his touch.

The same scar I'd seen on The Shade's lips when he had been as close to me as Elias was now.

FIVE

CEO and charismatic billionaire Elias Shaw was The Shade.

The Shade was walking around, pretending to be a normal human being.

That had to mean all the superhumans could assume human identities. What that implied for the rest of us, I couldn't even begin to imagine.

I groaned and leaned against the wall in the corridor I was hiding in, trying to still my mind's wild spinning by rubbing at my forehead.

I'd... *slow-danced* with The Shade.

Elias had asked if he could call me sometime, and I'd agreed, too intent on fleeing to pay much attention to what he was saying. It wasn't fear that'd made me hightail it out of the ballroom the second I could do so without rousing suspicion from anyone. No, it was the sheer magnitude of my discovery.

I knew The Shade's secret identity. No matter how much he claimed to want to protect me, I had no doubt that if he ever as much as suspected my newfound knowledge, I'd be dead. And, undoubtedly, he wasn't the only one who'd kill me for this secret. If Lightning found out I knew, I was pretty certain he'd do whatever he needed to to get it out of me.

Oh, God. Lightning's enemy was posing as his friend!

And who was Lightning then pretending to be, when he wasn't dressed up in a mask and a skintight suit? And Bright?

I rubbed harder at my forehead, wishing I'd never walked into that coffee shop where I'd run into Lightning. It seemed like the harder I fought to untangle the web of deceit and corruption, the more entangled I became.

There was only one thing for me to do, and that was continue with what I'd come here for. I needed to look for clues that could help explain the mayor's position in all of this—the rest of this giant headache would have to wait for later.

I pushed off the wall, intent on at least getting the information I'd come for.

FINDING the mayor's office without being detected was fairly easy. It was on the first floor by the end of the main hallway, and everyone—including security—was focused on the main entrance and the ballroom, where all the important guests were located. It wasn't even locked.

"I was so not born to be a spy," I muttered as I slipped into the office. It was as lavish as the rest of the mansion, and dominated by a big mahogany desk situated near the tall, curtained windows. The walls were lined with bookcases, and an exquisite sofa set was sprawled across the middle of the room.

I looked around, wondering where to start searching, when my gaze fell on the mayor's sleek computer monitor perched on the desk.

Well, everyone else kept all their information there...

Unfortunately, everyone also had password protection on their computers. At least everyone who didn't want others to rifle through their private affairs.

I stared at the taunting message on the screen, asking me to fill in the password. Okay, an unlocked door was probably as much luck as I was due on this adventure. Time to engage my Serious Reporter smarts.

"Password."

Wrong Password.

"password."

Wrong password.

"Password123," "PASSWORD," "pASSWORD,". "Wrong Password," "Evil_Overlord2000." "OpenSesame." "WhatAmIDoingWithMyLife."
"Who_Is_Bright_And_Why_Do_You_Want_To_Kill_Me?"

I paused for a moment, considering my last, denied suggestion. *I wonder...*

"Bright."

I had to bite my tongue to swallow a triumphant cheer when the image on the screen changed to desktop view. *Bright, huh?* And just why was the mayor using a supervillain's name as his password?

I searched through his files and folders as quickly as I could, dismissing the boring and legal-looking stuff. When I found a file labeled "alternative budget" I took pictures of the screen with my phone. The quicker I could get out of this office, the better, and this way I could look through everything in the privacy of my own home—without the constant risk of exposure and death looming over my head.

There were other suspicious-looking files too, and I snapped pictures of all of them, under the theory that too much material would be better than not enough. I also took pictures of all files that included the word "blue" in them, as per Aaron's recommendation, even though none of them looked remotely interesting. There were a lot of what looked like blueprints and schematics from city planning projects, but I faithfully photographed them all. Maybe there was some secret code hidden in the drawings, or something that would pop out upon further inspection.

I was just about to close everything down when a deep, angry voice made my heart leap into my throat.

"What do you think you're doing?"

My gaze shot up from the screen as a million scenarios of my impending demise flashed through my brain, but the person slipping into the office and closing the door behind him wasn't one of the mayor's goons. It was Lightning.

My breath whooshed out in a relieved sigh at the sight of the superhuman. "Thank God! You scared me."

"*Scared* you?" he hissed, his tall form descending on the desk I was sat behind with supernatural speed. "So you do have some sense of self-preservation? Because I gotta tell you, it doesn't look like you have any!"

The unmistakable anger in his gaze was unnerving. I was used to his sarcasm and teasing smirks—not a man with inhuman strength glaring at me like this.

"I was just looking for some proof, okay?" I turned off the computer and pushed out from the desk. "I needed to see if there was a connection between the mayor and—"

"You needed to stay out of this!" he interrupted with

something resembling a snarl. "I told you I'd take care of it, and here you are—not only traipsing around at the mayor's fucking ball like a goddamn lamb in a wolf's den, but also breaking into his office and snooping through his computer! What does it take for you to grasp the seriousness of the situation? If it had been anyone but me coming to look for you, you'd be dead. Do you understand? *Dead.*"

I swallowed. His mouth's angry slant and the rough, gravelly quality to his voice reminded me way too much of The Shade, and I didn't quite know what to do with it when it came from the normally irreverent hero.

"Why do you care so much what I do?" It probably wasn't the smartest question to ask an angry superhuman. In fact, when his eyes flashed and he grasped my shoulder a little too tightly, I *knew* it hadn't been the smart thing to ask.

"I put my mark on you, you little dimwit," he growled, and something other than anger moved behind his gaze. It was another emotion that reminded me all too well about The Shade. Dark possessiveness. Without my brain's permission, my panties turned damp.

Great. Fucking great. Why was I such a slut for caveman behavior?

"You belong to *me.* And if another superhuman sees my mark on the pretty little girl who was sneaking around where she shouldn't be, they'll assume *I* sent you. Do you have any idea what kind of ramifications that would have?"

My own anger rose sharp and hot. It wasn't even concern for my safety that had him yelling at me like I was a slow child—it was how it could implicate him! When he hadn't been there to protect me in the first place, even though he'd promised me he would.

I opened my mouth to give him a piece of my mind, but

just as I hissed, *"Now you listen here, buddy,"* in my best attempt at sounding intimidating, Lightning's head snapped to the side.

"Someone's coming," he mumbled.

I had just enough time to feel my anger transform into terror before I was suddenly on my back on the sofa with Lightning on top of me.

"What?" I squeaked. Lightning silenced my protests by pressing his lips against mine. His hot tongue flicked out, licking over the seam of my mouth. I'd like to say that it was sheer surprise that made me part my lips and invite him in.

He kissed me with such passion and ferociousness that I didn't realize what his hands were doing until cool air tightened my right nipple and his leather-clad fingers brushed my panties aside.

I jolted underneath him, shock and—shamefully— desire making me jerk away from the kiss. Lightning responded by dipping his mouth to my fully exposed breast, flicking the nipple once and then sucking it into his hot mouth.

"Ooh!"

It was at that point my body decided to take over. Sharp tendrils of pleasure rocked through me as Lightning sucked me deeply and rhythmically, punctuated by the brush of soft leather against my clit. My breath came in short pants under the hero's ministrations, and I arched my hips and spread my thighs, my wanton body only focused on getting more of this, more of *him*. When he slipped a single finger down through my soaked folds and up inside of me, I moaned.

"Ahem."

The sharp voice made my brain return, its arrival sending an unpleasant shock of embarrassment through me as I looked up at the three men crowding the doorway. Staring at us.

Lightning lifted up from my breast, his mouth making a loud, wet pop as it left my erect nipple before he turned his head to glance over his shoulder at the newcomers. His gloved finger stayed lodged in my pussy, drawing light patterns against my walls.

"Ah, mayor. Do you need the office?"

"Well, I was planning on showing Mr. Hemsworth and Mr. Billington my collection of antique ledgers, but far be it from me to interrupt a romantic rendezvous. Even a hero can feel in need of a woman's embrace, I presume."

"We can indeed, but I'm sure Miss Smith will be amenable to changing locations. What do you say, Kathryn? Wanna let the mayor get on with his business?" Lightning's gaze slid back to mine, perfect innocence—as if nothing was amiss—shining from it.

I only managed a humiliated squeak in response.

"I think that's a yes. If you'd just give us a moment to let the lady get presentable?"

"Naturally. A lady must retain her dignity." The word "lady" was dripping with sarcasm. "We'll be in the drawing room, looking at the Monét."

The second the door closed behind the mayor and his guests, I pushed Lightning off me, slapping at his arm until he pulled his finger from my pussy. The leather was covered in a wet shine.

"What the hell!" I hissed, shame tightening my throat. "What do you think you're doing, mauling me like a lustful bear! I can't even...! Oh, God, what they must *think!*"

"They think we snuck in here for a quick fuck, which is quite a bit better than the alternative, don't you agree?"

He had a point, sure, but I wasn't ready to admit to that—
not even close. Instead of answering, I managed to get into a
seated position so I could push my bra back over my exposed
breast, rearrange the dress' shoulder strap, and then bend to
sort out the wardrobe malfunction lower down.

I'd just managed to get my panties back in place when a
low growl filled the room. It was dark and threatening, and
filled with a primal fury. Cold chills ran down my spine and
every hair on my body stood on end as I whipped my head
around to look at the source—at Lightning.

His gaze had turned terrifyingly animalistic—and it was
fixed on *me*.

I gulped, pausing my hands' attempt at straightening out
my skirt. "L-Lightning?"

"*What. Is. That?*"

Before I could ask what he was on about, he'd grabbed
the back of my neck, fingers pressing against the place The
Shade had bitten me.

Oh. Fuck. I'd had my hair in curls cascading down my
back for the event, effectively hiding the mark from superhuman eyes, but bending down just now had bared it for
Lightning.

"That's—" I began, intent on explaining how I'd had no
choice, but I was interrupted by a deep snarl.

"I know what the fuck it is! What I don't know is how
The-fucking-Shade's mark happens to be placed on *my*
woman's neck! And the fucker had the audacity to place it *on
top of mine!* I am going to *murder* him!"

Whoa. While I'd been pretty certain Lightning wouldn't
be thrilled about The Shade metaphorically peeing on his
property, I'd had no idea the response would be this violent.

"Calm down, he—"

"He had no fucking right!" Lightning interrupted me with a hiss. "And *you!* Parting your legs for that scumbag! Did you like being fucked like a common whore? Is that why you let him mark you? Because I didn't give you the cock you so desperately crave?"

And just like that, my instinctive fear turned into explosive anger.

"No, I let him mark me because I didn't have a goddamn choice!" I just about managed to keep my voice low enough that we wouldn't be overheard by the mayor and the two men he'd been with, but oh, how I wanted to scream into the arrogant idiot's masked face. "He saved me from the mayor's men when they tried to rape and kidnap me, and this is what he wanted in return. If it's such a big fucking deal to you, maybe you should have been around to protect me like you said you would! He was there—you weren't. So yeah, you know what? I'd much rather fuck him than you—at least he keeps his word and actually gives a shit whether I live or die."

I got up off the couch, snatched my clutch off the floor, and stomped over to the door, too furious to care if my clothes were ruffled or not. The anger still boiling in my gut, I spun around and snarled, "And it was really fucking good!" before I left the office, slamming the door.

SIX

I was still so angry I was shaking when I sat down in front of my computer to write a fluff piece about the ball. As much as I wanted to spend the night raging about how unbelievably rude Lightning had been, I needed to get a blog post about all the pretty dresses and expensive paintings up as soon as possible. Doing so would go a long way to placating the mayor, if he was still suspicious of me, and it might help me get some more blog traffic, too. As unimportant as the Autumn Ball was for the general population of St. Anthony, people still loved to look at pictures and gossip about all the important people who attended. And who was I to say no to free money?

After losing my heels and changing into my faithful footie pajamas, I'd managed to get absorbed in my work when one of the pictures I'd uploaded made me pause.

Elias Shaw, CEO and elusive billionaire stared back at me, champagne glass in hand.

Somehow, the blow-out with Lightning had made me forget what else I'd discovered that evening.

The question was, what was I going to do about it?

He had protected me and gone out of his way to ensure the mayor didn't find me suspicious, and my body yearned for him whenever he was close, whether he wore his disguise or not. But The Shade was also a very, very bad man. Even if only half the rumors about him were true, the city as a whole would be safer if he was locked up somewhere. Hadn't I seen with my own eyes how he could kill without thinking twice?

Of course, I had only seen him murder someone to defend me. The mark throbbed, as if in agreement.

I cursed the part of me that instinctively came to his defense and rubbed the back of my neck. That blasted mark had caused enough trouble for one night.

Maybe I could talk to him about it. Not the fact that I knew who he was posing as during the day, obviously, but about the rumors circulating about him. If I knew for certain that he was evil to the core, then perhaps I could think more about revealing who he was to someone who could take him down. Even if the part of me mind-controlled by my ovaries protested violently at the thought.

Sudden tendrils of awareness tickled down my spine, and I stiffened in my seat at the now all-too-familiar sensation.

Someone was in my apartment with me. Again.

I snapped my head around to glare over my shoulder at the kitchen.

"*Really?* Again?" I huffed, fully expecting to see The Shade emerge from the shadows. "Can't you use the goddamn doorbell like a normal person?"

"This is easier," came the calm answer from somewhere behind my counter. A red-and-charcoal-clad figure stepped into the faint light cast by my desk lamp, and I bit my lip to avoid voicing my surprise. Lightning probably wouldn't take too kindly to the fact that I'd expected his enemy.

"It's also ruder," I snapped. His comments from earlier still rang clear in my mind. *Masked asshole.* "What do you want?"

"I came to apologize." He moved smoothly across the floor and sat on my desk, ignoring the daggers I was glaring at him. "I was... surprised, and I said some things I shouldn't have."

"Damn right you shouldn't." I moved back a bit so I could look up at him without craning my neck too much. "What right do you have to judge me like that?"

A touch of the primal anger from before flashed in his eyes, but this time I recognized it for what is also was. From what I'd seen in The Shade's gaze. Possessiveness.

He forced it down, opting for an apologetic look instead. "I'm sorry I said those things to you. And that I didn't explain... better, about the mark and what it means. Truth be told, I didn't truly understand it myself, until... until I saw *his* mark on you. But most of all, I'm sorry you had to submit to him. I claimed you, and I should have been there to protect you."

My own anger withered at the sincerity in his voice. Unless he was a frighteningly good actor, he meant what he said.

I nodded once, to show my acceptance of his apology. "Thanks."

A small smile pulled the corner of his mouth up. "You know, other girls would have climbed me like a tree after a heartfelt apology, and you just say 'thanks'?"

And there we were again, right back to him being an insufferable ass.

I narrowed my eyes. "Other girls don't know what an arrogant jerk you truly are. Or perhaps you use that mind control thing on them, who knows?"

His smile widened. "Ah, there you are. I did miss your wicked little tongue tonight. There are surprisingly few humans who will give a superhuman attitude."

"Perhaps because you mind rape the ones that do?" My tone was still more than a little sharp.

"You're just never gonna let that go, are you?" he hummed. "We can't mind control people, you know. It's just that you find our pheromones rather appealing, and we can ramp them up a bit when the situation requires it."

I blinked, baffled that he was sharing information about his kind with me. As far as I knew, no one had any knowledge about superhuman *pheromones*. "So you can't make people do what you want?"

Lightning scoffed. "Well, not unless they're female and already have at least a small sexual interest in me. And then I can mainly just get them to bang." His smile turned wicked. "Don't get me wrong, it's a very useful skill. But if I could simply mind control people I'd just ask the mayor what he's up to, not attend his boring parties and pretend like I give a flying fuck about his art collection."

"Oh. Is that what you are doing? Trying to find an in with him?"

He sighed, stretching his long limbs as if he was particularly tired after the Autumn Ball. "Yup. As long as he sees me as a friend, he won't suspect I'm looking into his affairs. And neither will anyone else. Which, of course, is just another reason you need to keep your lovely, round ass out of trouble."

I ignored the comment about my ample backside. "And why are you telling me this?"

"Apart from trying to stop you from breaking into the mayor's office another time? Because it's my responsibility to take care of you, and maybe by explaining things a bit better, I can stop you from rushing head-first into whatever trouble you can find."

I eyed him suspiciously. "What, exactly, do you mean by it being your responsibility to take care of me?"

"You're mine." A flash of the anger from before filtered through his blue gaze. "*I* protect you. Not that fucking pickpocket who thought he could come in and *erase* my mark."

"Oh. Right." I didn't have the nerve to tell him that, if The Shade had marked me to get under his skin, then it was working. "Does that mean you'll tell me what the heck is going on?"

Lightning sent me a long glance. "I can't tell you everything. You're a human, and there are rules. But I can tell you that whatever Wilkins is involved in, it's somehow linked to the supe community. There has been a shift in our ranks, and there are whispers of something big going down soon. I don't know what yet, but whenever there are secrets circulating, it's never good. What I'm dying to know is how Wilkins is involved. My gut instinct tells me he's deeper into it than simply bankrolling the supe leaders with city funds, but *how* exactly they're using him, I don't know." He raised his chin at me, lips slipping into a soft quirk. "You didn't happen to stumble across any leads while messing around on his computer, did you?"

The tone suggested he was half-joking, and I hurriedly shook my head. I'd yet to look through the pictures I'd taken, and in case there actually was something on there, I'd want to see it myself before he or The Shade yanked it from me. "Nuh-uh. Nothing of interest."

"Figured," Lightning sighed, finally hopping down off my desk. "He's too slippery to get caught redhanded. But never mind—I don't want you worrying yourself over any of this going forward, understood? Your little gamble seems to have paid off, meaning you're no longer at risk as far as Wilkins goes. So no more getting yourself into trouble, hm?"

I wondered if he knew just how much he sounded like his archenemy when he went all "primitive protector" on me. Then, when his pointed gaze indicated he wanted a response from me, I nodded seriously, giving him as honest a facial expression as I could muster.

"Of course not. I just wanted to be safe. If the mayor and whoever else might have thought I was a threat are pacified after tonight, I'm out."

I wasn't out, not by a long shot. I'd been pulled way too far into this to just tap out, even if I believed that no one would ever try to hurt me for that damn article again. Not after what happened with Peter Miller, and the promise I'd made to Aaron. But I was fairly certain that saying anything along those lines to the superhuman staring at me wouldn't be in my best interests.

"You wouldn't be lying to me, would you, Kittykat?"

"Of course not." I managed an expression of hurt at his accusation. "Do you think I find it fun to be chased through the streets by a pack of goons? I just want my life to go back to normal."

"Fair enough. Then I presume you don't mind if I look through your phone? See what sort of pictures you took tonight?"

Fuck.

"Of course not." I handed him the device, because if I didn't he would know I'd lied. "Though that's pretty violating, just so you know—a masked vigilante demanding to rifle through citizens' phones."

He gave me a short glance before flicking through to my photos. "You're not a citizen—you're *mine*. Be happy I asked you. That's not how most of these bonds work."

"What do you mean?" I asked, genuinely affronted. He made it sound like I was some sort of... slave. An unpleasant sense of foreboding nestled in my gut.

"I mean that most humans who are marked by a supe become little more than his property." Lightning didn't even bother looking up from my phone as his words made icy tendrils travel up my spine.

"*What?* You—are you saying you see me as your *property?* That is so fucked up! I can tell you right now, that's not happening, buddy!"

Lightning snorted, eyes still glued to my phone's screen. "No, I'm saying that's what normally happens. I have no idea why you're different. You just are. When I saw you crouched under a table in that coffee shop, I knew there was something... unique about you. I've never claimed a human before, yet you—I wanted to mark your neck from the first time you opened your mouth."

I blinked. "Uh... what... does that mean?"

He looked up at me then, and there was not an ounce of hesitation or sarcasm in his glowing gaze. "It means you're mine, Kathryn. *Mine.* It means I had to fight every goddamn instinct in my body not to flip you over and fuck you raw when I saw The Shade's mark on you. It means I will protect you with my own flesh if need be."

That... didn't even come close to answering any of my

questions. In fact, it only gave birth to more as I stared at the dark possessiveness in the superhuman's eyes. More questions and a hot pulse low in my abdomen that seemed to spread up through my body for every second his gaze was locked in mine.

Dammit. Why did Neanderthal behavior get to me like this?

Lightning finally broke eye contact, looking back down on my phone without another word. I was quiet for several moments while my dazed brain tried to come to grips with his words and their disturbing effect on my body. Then the image of Elias Shaw flicked over the screen, and I was jolted out of my stupor. If I wanted to keep whatever I'd found on the mayor's computer for myself until I'd had a chance at sorting through it—and not get caught in a lie—then I needed to distract him. Now.

"Why didn't you have sex with me?" The words seemed to just fall out of my mouth on their own before I managed to clamp my lips shut around them. A hefty flush shot into my cheeks when Lightning raised his gaze once more.

"Beg your pardon?" His soft tone was in complete contrast to the searing heat of his darkened eyes.

I gulped, instinctively licking my lips. "You, ah, said you wanted to... at the mayor's office. Why didn't you?"

"Did you want me to?"

Well... that wasn't exactly the reply I'd imagined. I blinked and cleared my throat. "T-that wasn't what I meant."

"Oh?" Finally, he put my phone down. Only it didn't ease any of the tension in my pulsing body. Lightning closed the small gap between us with steps as smooth as a stalking feline and, when he was right in front of me and my heart was pounding, bent down with one hand on each armrest of my chair, closing me in.

"Tell me then, Kittykat. What did you mean?"

"Just that... The Shade said a claim wasn't valid without sex, and... and you didn't sleep with me when you marked me, either. I just don't understand why."

His eyes narrowed at the mention of his enemy. "I think I told you, the last time I was in your apartment. You may not think I'm the hero the rest of the city believes in, but *I* don't force women to submit to me. Unless, of course, they ask me to."

My heart thudded erratically when he lowered his gaze from my eyes to my lips, only to slowly raise it again.

"Are you asking?"

The sensible part of my brain wanted to say no, because despite all his rippling abs and wicked smile, I knew he wasn't the hero he postured as. I *knew* I needed to back away from the heat in his eyes before I was consumed.

Unfortunately, the sensible part of my brain wasn't currently in control. When I mindlessly leaned forward and pressed my lips to his, my ovaries were in the driver's seat.

Lightning growled low in his throat when my mouth pressed against his, and as the lush flavor of his kiss washed over my senses his strong hands landed on my hips, pulling me up from the chair and flush against his firm body as if I weighed nothing.

I moaned incoherently into his mouth, too wrapped up in the electric currents racing underneath my skin. His tongue swept in between my parted lips and delved deeper, and I melted in against his powerful frame.

The hands on my hips stroked up, easily finding the buttons in my footie pajamas without ever breaking the kiss.

But when he'd opened all the buttons and lifted his hands to brush it off my shoulders, my apprehension reared its ugly head. With The Shade I hadn't been naked, and despite the intoxication of Lightning's desire, my brain suddenly filled with images of his eyes on my soft, imperfect body.

When my hands found his and stopped their attempt to rid me of my clothes, Lightning broke the kiss. He looked down at me questioningly, and I felt a humiliated blush spread up my chest to my face.

"I'm sorry, it's just..." I fumbled with the front of my footie pajamas, trying to button it up again. His hands paused my attempt.

"No." It was a borderline growl. "I want to see all of you."

I flinched, trying to shy away, but Lightning was determined. He pushed my hands away and pulled at the fabric covering my shoulders, letting it slide down my torso. My nipples tightened at the sudden exposure to the air, and I made a vain attempt to hide behind my arms while Lightning yanked the footie pajamas over my hips, grabbing my panties on the way down and letting both pool at my feet.

"Let me see you." It was a flat-out command.

I wasn't normally too bothered by my rounded figure, so why did I feel this way now? Just because the man in front of me was physical perfection, just because no one had seen me fully naked in years... I did my best to silence the inner panic and, reluctantly, lowered my arms and raised my chin up in defiance.

The low, rich growl that vibrated out of Lightning's chest made my pulse throb for something entirely different than embarrassment, and I felt the heated knot in my abdomen melt as moisture began to seep from my core.

He reached out, grabbing my hips hard, but when his leather-clad hands touched my skin he pulled back with a grunt. With swift movements he yanked off his gloves, only to grasp me by the hips once more. His touch was as heated as his kiss had been when his fingers dug into my flesh, pulling me close.

"Don't ever hide that beautiful body from me again." Lightning's voice was hoarse and deep, its rumble echoing deep inside of me. "Do you understand?"

I nodded slowly, too dazed by the desire thrumming through my body to object. In his eyes I saw no judgment of my imperfections, nor disappointment—only a *deep, fiery need*. It turned me on like nothing before it.

Of their own accord my hands reached for his suit, fumbling for a zipper or buttons—anything to get to his skin. I needed to feel it under my fingertips, needed to stroke my hands over his firm muscles and know that he was really there.

Lightning chuckled and reached behind his back, undoing the top part of his two-toned suit. When he stripped it off, I could barely grasp the magnitude of his masculinity. Every single muscle in his chest, arms, and stomach were clearly defined and thickly coiled around his tall frame. A smattering of hair trailed down his lightly bronzed skin below his navel, disappearing behind his crimson-and-charcoal pants that clung to the pronounced "V" of his hips like a second skin.

"*Oh, wow.*"

I wasn't even aware of my own breathy appreciation before Lightning's lips quirked up in response. Then his hands returned to my body, and my brain tapped out.

He was like a firestorm, embracing me with scorching

heat and bruising strength emphasized by featherlight brushes of his fingertips as he rounded every one of my body's curves.

"I need more of you," he whispered hoarsely against my ear, sweeping his hands up over my soft stomach to cup my full breasts. "How do you do this to me? I'm aching to be inside of you."

I groaned an agreement, and then moaned when his mouth dipped to my left nipple, sucking it deep into his mouth. The firestorm turned electric, and I arched into him as his teasing suckles went straight to my clit, making it ache and throb for attention. I reached out for him, letting my hands roam over his chiseled chest, and was rewarded with another rich growl that vibrated against my palms.

His mouth came off my nipple with a wet pop, but instead of going straight for the other, he reached down and grabbed my ass, lifting me up so I was forced to part my thighs for his hips. Before I managed much more than a squeak, I was on my back on my bed, staring dumbfounded up at the smirking superhuman.

"Lightning speed," was his only comment. "Let me show you what else it's good for."

Faster than my eyes could track he'd knelt between my still-spread thighs, and then his mouth pressed against my slit.

I gasped and grasped at the sheets, because without pausing he delved his tongue in between my parted flesh, licking broadly from my entrance to the pearl up top.

"*God!*" My outburst was followed by immediate panting and thrashing as his tongue lashed at my clit from every possible angle, faster than my nerves could even fully comprehend. The result was a whirlwind of sensation bursting through my poor nub and into my bloodstream where it overloaded my entire system. I was faintly aware that I was screaming like a banshee, but I was way too far gone to care. The desire that had been smoldering in my abdomen since he first entered my apartment was set free and running rampant through my body, rising up through my squirming spine like a tsunami.

My orgasm struck before I'd even realized it was building.

"Yes! Fuck! God, yes!" I clutched at his head as I crashed over the edge, pressing my thighs tight around his neck as my body rode it out. Only the merciless lashings against my clit never allowed me to ebb, and as if someone flicked a switch, the stimulation turned agonizing.

"Stop, please, God, stop! No more!" I wailed my plea out while flailing desperately in Lightning's iron grip, but I might as well have attempted to dislodge a mountain. Thankfully, he stopped on his own, giving my pulsing clit a gentle kiss before lifting his gaze to mine.

"I asked if you wanted me to make you submit," he said, his rich voice drifting over my mound and abdomen in a warm caress. "I do hope you don't think we're done now—or you are in for a rude awakening."

I groaned and let my head fall down on the sheets I'd crumpled up in my fitful orgasm. "Human here... remember!" I gasped, trying to control the tremors still rippling through my body. "You need... to slow down!"

Lightning's smirk turned decidedly wicked. "Why? I enjoy seeing you struggle to take all the pleasure I can give your beautiful little body." Another kiss landed on my clit, and another, followed by gentle suction. I moaned and lifted my hips, caught between needing to rest and wanting to chase the slow burn of pleasure he stirred once again.

Lightning didn't give me much of a choice.

The gentle sucking turned more insistent, and I forgot I'd wanted a break. Bursts of pleasure burned through my nerves, but he was gentler this time, letting me climb toward my peak at a steady pace rather than rushing me forward. When two of his fingers dipped into my pussy and curved for my g-spot, my moans and gasps turned to sharp whines and yelps. He finger-fucked me deep and fast, forcing my hips to buck up against his demanding mouth.

"*Lightning!*" I pleaded, not even fully conscious that my grasping hands were tugging roughly on the mask covering the top half of his head. "More, more, *more!*"

I felt rather than heard his chuckle vibrate against my clit. Then he flattened his tongue against my aching nub and pressed in hard, while forcing a third finger into my clenching channel.

I came so hard I nearly blacked out from the flood of pleasure assaulting my mind and body in one intense climax.

"So demanding."

The deep voice seemed to float from somewhere above me. I opened my eyes and smiled hazily at the masked man bent over my splayed form.

"Remember how you begged for more when I fuck you again and again and again." He leaned forward further, catching my lips in a deep kiss as he braced his weight on his hands next to my head. I tasted my own slickness on his lips, the heady tang driving home how perfectly depraved this night was.

I spread my legs wider and lifted up my pelvis to grind against his hard stomach, emboldened by the rush of endorphins bathing my mind and body. "So much talk, big hero... So little fucking."

Lightning flashed me a wicked grin and pulled back up to undo his pants. "You really need to learn to watch that lip, little human." A streak of red blurred in front of me, and suddenly the superhuman was kneeling on the bed, naked and *hard*. "One of these days, it'll get you into some real big trouble."

In a perfect world, I'd have shot his crude banter down with a smart comeback. But then again, in a perfect world, my lover wouldn't be aiming an erection that looked like it belonged on a medium sized pony at me.

"Holy fuck!" My pussy contracted involuntarily, moisture seeping down my slit in either anticipation or terror. I'd never seen a cock that big—not even in porn. It must have been a good ten inches long and easily wider than my wrist.

"Indeed." He fell down on top of me again, caging me in with his granite arms. "I've been aching for this since the first time I saw you. Your body drives me crazy—so soft and fragile and *human*."

The darkness in his voice made me look up and into his eyes. Gone was the playful arrogance and the teasing. Only dark, primal *lust* stared back at me.

"*Oh!*" My exclamation pitched when he grabbed my hamstrings and lifted my legs up and apart, leaving me exposed and defenseless. He slid his hands up my inner thighs, keeping them spread wide for him, only to finally descend on my sopping pussy with a purely animalistic *growl*.

Lightning opened me up, spreading my lower lips so nothing was between him and my quivering entrance.

My heart pounded with equal measures of lust and

apprehension. He was so big, and what I'd seen in his eyes just now—something so far from humanity my mind struggled to grasp its significance—scared me on an instinctive level. Buried deep in my reptilian brain, something was screaming about dangerous predators, but it couldn't drown out how wet and ready my body was for him. How much I ached for him.

When his thick cock sank in between my pussy lips, my eyes rolled back in their sockets from relief. The heavy pressure centered the mounting thrill and focused my entire being on that one, single sensation of his warm flesh against mine.

Then he flexed his hips and drove in, and the sensation crescendoed from pure elation to a roiling turmoil of wild pleasure, intense, stretching pressure, and a sliver of pain.

"*God,* go slow!" I gasped and fumbled at his chest while my pussy struggled to take the brutal stretch. The last time I'd felt this full, I hadn't had a chance to protest the size before the massive cock was fully embedded inside of me. Lightning went slower than The Shade had, but not nearly slow enough. All I could fully comprehend, all I could feel, was his girth forcing my poor pussy to submit, inch after merciless inch.

"No," he growled above me. I moaned as he grabbed my hands in one of his and pinned them above my head. "You don't get to make demands now. Your tight little cunt is *my* domain—I am in charge now, baby, and you will surrender to me." And with that, he pushed in to the hilt in one long, smooth thrust.

I screamed.

It only hurt for a moment, my wetness allowing for his penetration without causing any serious pain. The overwhelming feeling of being filled—*taken*—to the brim, however, was unyielding.

Lightning grunted hoarsely as he paused, fully seated inside of me, and pressed a kiss to my parted lips. I opened my eyes when his mouth left mine and gasped at the feral expression in his eyes. He released my jaw and shifted so he could entwine his fingers with mine while still keeping my arms locked above my head. And then he moved.

"Lightning...!"

I dug my fingernails into the grooves of his knuckles as hard as I could, needing something, anything, to anchor me to reality while my pussy clamped down around his thick length. The bulging rim of his mushroom head dragged against my g-spot, only to shove it roughly back when he reversed the movement to once again fill me. There was nothing in the world but his cock, nothing but his long, slick thrusts and my spasming pussy being penetrated deep and hard.

I wailed for each time he bottomed out in me, but when he finally released my hands to grab my hips so he could increase the pace, I had no intention of trying to get free from underneath him. Instead, I clutched on to his back and bit down on his shoulder to stem my screams as Lightning sped up.

He lied when he said he wouldn't go slow before, because in comparison to *this*—he had been gentle.

The hero pounded my soaking pussy harder and faster than any human could have hoped to replicate, the brutal force demanding my full submission. It didn't take long for my body to comply, too overcome with the sheer power of his thrusts to object.

My pussy clenched hard around the invasion, and as it did, Lightning pressed a thumb to my clit and rubbed.

The tight coil in my core snapped at the dual assault, and I cried out in a guttural outburst as I came, my pussy milking his thick shaft.

Lightning paused and rested inside of me while I came down. Light touches to my face followed by a soft kiss on my lips made me look up at him in time to see the hot possessiveness in his glowing eyes. It made warmth spread in my chest—something I thankfully had no ability to dwell on too much in my post-orgasmic haze and with Lightning's hard and demanding cock still lodged inside.

"Ready for more, lover?"

Even in my blissed-out state, I couldn't hold back an amused snort. "Do I have a choice?"

His grin was decidedly dark. "No."

"Good." I wrapped my legs around his lower back and my arms around his neck, pulling him down close. As much as I'd regret it in the morning, some deep, depraved part of me was craving to be fucked until I had nothing left to give.

Lightning rolled his hips and I gasped, biting down hard on my lip as he bottomed out again. He tangled his hands in my hair, pulling my head back so he could trace my exposed throat with his lips and teeth while he drove into me.

My tight sheath clung to him for each thrust, but my body accommodated him more easily now. The thick rim of his head felt like pure ecstasy as it rubbed my g-spot over and over, and the wet noises and hoarse grunts filling my loft only fueled my pleasure.

Just when a new orgasm began to build, Lightning changed position.

He grabbed me by the hips, pulled out, and flipped me

over to my stomach. I squealed in surprise, only to whimper when he grabbed a handful of my hair and pulled so I was forced up on my hands and knees, neck arched back. That was all the warning I had before Lightning pushed in between my soaked folds and forced himself inside of me.

I grunted as his heavy balls slapped my pussy lips, the new position making me feel him even more keenly than before. His grip on my hair stopped me from shifting forward to ease the pressure in my pussy, leaving me no choice but to take it. All of it.

When he started thrusting, I abandoned all attempts of holding back my screams. I yowled and cried and tore at the bedding while he fucked into me so fast and rough the bed banged against the wall hard enough for the whitewash to peel off the bricks and crumble to the floor. Somewhere in the torrent of pleasure and delicious agony I knew that *this* was the real sex—this was what he'd been waiting for while pleasuring and preparing my body. He wasn't human, and nothing about this fucking was human, either.

His snarls of pleasure made a steady undertone for my loud wails, while the *thwack* of his thighs against my ass and hamstrings punctuated the brutal rhythm he was pounding me with.

Only when he released my hair and pressed his hand against my clit did my focus sway from the ruthless penetration. Lightning pinched my little nub until it throbbed, and then rubbed it as hard and fast as he was fucking me.

My responding scream pitched higher than before, and I bucked to try and escape the too-intense stimulation.

Lightning didn't budge, keeping me firmly in place while never letting up the thrusts into my spasming pussy, and eventually, my body caved. The sharps shocks turned to burning pleasure and I pressed down for more, inadvertently tilting my hips in the process. His next thrust went straight into my g-spot, and I saw stars.

My climax came like a flood, breaking the banks of my mind and drowning me with pure, raw sensation. There was nothing but sharp, powerful pleasure and darkness for what felt like an eternity.

Then a hard sting at the nape of my neck ripped me back to reality. A reality where I was screaming until my throat was raw, and my body twitched and spasmed underneath the heavy press of the man lying on top of me, pinning me to the mattress. Warm semen pulsed inside of me, milked from the thick cock now slowly rocking back and forth against my cervix.

When I finally stopped coming, Lightning stilled on top of me. He released my neck from his bite and wrapped his big body around my backside, completely covering my damp skin, and gently nuzzled against my cheek.

"You okay?"

"Mmhm." I was more than okay. I was completely spent and sore in places that had only ever been reached once before, but the afterbuzz of my violent orgasm and the feel of his strong body protecting me from everything and everyone far overshadowed my exhaustion.

Lightning kissed my cheek and earlobe at my confirmation that he hadn't irreparably broken any important parts of me, and then nuzzled at the bite mark he'd left on my neck. I groaned, annoyed at the slight sting, and then sighed with pleasure as he began soothing it with long, slow licks. My eyes drifted shut to the sound of a soft rumble vibrating from his chest and into my lax body.

SEVEN

I think I dozed off for a bit, because when I opened my eyes again, I was curled up on my side with an arm and a leg splayed over Lightning's naked body. He had an arm hooked around my back and was stroking his other hand through my tangled hair, much like one would pet a sleeping cat.

"That was amazing," I mumbled. I pressed my nose against his neck and inhaled his delicious musk. Why did even his smell make my body hum?

His arm constricted around me for a moment, pulling me closer to him, but he didn't answer.

The unusual quietude made me glance up to see his soft lips pinched to a narrow line.

"Lightning? Is something wrong?"

His eyes flickered down to meet mine. A glimmer of unease swirled in their blue depths.

"Not a thing, Kittykat. Go back to sleep."

So that was a lie. I blinked, my brain slowly pulling itself from the foggy depths of pleasure-induced sleep in alarm.

With some effort, I raised up on an elbow so I could glare down at his still-masked face.

"Don't you try to lie to me. Don't you think we're past that by now?" I made a sweeping motion over our entangled bodies.

Lightning scoffed. "You think every girl I fuck gets to know my secrets?"

The words were like a slap. I reeled back, grabbing for the covers to hide my naked form. "What did you just say?"

He sighed and pushed up into a half-seated position, resting on both elbows. "Look, don't take it personally. I know the mark makes you susceptible to all sorts of *feelings*, but that doesn't mean anything. I'm not your boyfriend, and we're not going to do the whole 'post-coital conversation.' "

Anger welled up to compete with the unexpected hurt blooming in my chest, caused by the man who had just spent a few hours making me feel so wonderful and safe. I'd not as much as mentioned any type of possible commitment, and—

Hang on.

The *mark.*

The goddamn mark.

I reached for the back of my neck where the remnants of his bite throbbed unpleasantly, as if it was agitated by my anger.

He'd bitten me. Again. He'd only fucked me so he could mark and claim me fully.

Realization made the anger tip into absolute rage. I lifted my hand and brought it down on his chest before I even knew what I was doing. The sting in my palm felt good—it distracted me from the betrayal threatening to overwhelm my heart.

"Get out!"

"Kathryn—"

"*Get. Out.* You come in here and think you can use me in your pissing contest with The Shade? And then you dismiss me, because you think I have *feelings* for you? I'm not the one who's determined to claim ownership over *you*, am I? So get the *fuck* out of my apartment, and don't you dare come back! I am not a thing you can own, and I am done with you. You hear? *Done!* Get out!"

For a moment we were staring at each other, and through my anger and hurt I thought I saw something... almost pained in the depths of his eyes. Then he nodded once, and the air around the bed swiveled red, blurring my vision. When I blinked, it was over. And Lightning was gone.

I CRIED. I cried, and I hated myself for it.

He didn't deserve my tears, nor the dull sense of betrayal and hurt in the pit of my stomach. He was right—he wasn't my boyfriend, and even before he'd told me I was just another girl he'd fucked, I hadn't liked him all that much. Falling into bed with him was just the result of a night filled with adrenaline spikes and the pheromones superhumans exuded—nothing else.

So why was my chest so hollow and sore from our confrontation?

I rubbed irritably at the mark. Maybe he was right— maybe the damn thing did mess with my emotions. It was still throbbing uncomfortably, an ever-present reminder of Lightning.

I finally gave up trying to fall asleep, wrapped my top blanket around my body, and padded barefoot to the freezer. Once I'd stocked up on chocolate ice cream, I plopped down on my sofa and turned on the TV. If anything could get my head straight again, it was mindless nighttime TV and a pint of Ben & Jerry's.

And that's how The Shade found me about an hour later.

"Hello, Kathryn."

I jolted from my nest of blankets and chocolate drips and whipped my head around in time to see his dark figure step out of the shadows.

Maybe I should have been scared at the sight of him, or at the very least a little anxious, but after the onslaught of emotions this night had brought, I didn't have any more angst left in me.

"Hello," I sighed before turning back around to the TV. "Whatever you're here for, I'm really not in the mood."

Only silence met my less than thrilled greeting, but I could sense him move behind me.

"You are unhappy." His voice sounded right above my head, and I couldn't help but tip my head back at the sound. He leaned forward, bracing both hands on the back of my sofa so he could stare down into my eyes. "Why?"

"It's just been a bad night. What do you want?" I had no desire to explain my encounter with Lightning to The Shade, so even though I was completely out of coping ability when it came to superhumans, I still tried to turn his attention back on whatever had made him break into my home this time.

Unfortunately, it didn't work.

"Did the mayor harm you?"

I shook my head. "No. Your plan worked brilliantly—he, and everyone else at that party, thought I was a complete dimwit. I'm even writing an article fawning over all the pretty dresses and artificially whitened smiles to solidify my reputation as an airhead. I'm good, really."

"You're not," he simply stated. When I straightened my neck back up again, his gloved finger on my chin pushed my head back so we could keep eye contact. "You're also naked."

The change of direction momentarily confused me—long enough for his eyes to narrow ever so slightly at my silence. And then he was crouched on the sofa next to me, pushing the blanket around my shoulders to the side.

"Hey, stop that!" I swatted at his hands to preserve some modesty, but he didn't try to yank the entire thing off me. Once my shoulder was exposed, he dipped his head and inhaled deeply at the spot where my shoulder and neck joined. The deep growl that followed made all the small hairs on my body stand on end.

"I smell Lightning all over you." The angry tone wasn't accusatory, nor was it a question. "Did he force you?"

"No, of course he didn't force me!" Perhaps I should have lied and said he did. The Shade had made it plenty clear that he considered me *his*. But the sheer ridiculousness of his question made the truth burst out before I'd even had a chance to think about the consequences.

"Then why are you upset?"

I blinked in surprise at his lack of anger at me—it all seemed to be directed at Lightning, and at the fact that I was "upset." In what fucked up world did the villain care if I was upset?

"Why do you care so much?" I shot back. "To you, I'm just a purchased good—nothing more than your whore, really. Lightning told me how a claim works for you supes."

The Shade's nostrils pulled up in obvious disgust. "It's nothing that simple."

"Really? You call me 'yours,' like I'm something you own, and think you can make demands of who I see and where I go."

"I protect you. That's entirely different."

Annoyance rose in my gut, burst through my chest, and came out my throat in a bitter laugh. "Yeah, right. Because you are such a *good guy, Mr. Murderer-of-Innocents*. It's not like we call you The Shade because of your black suit. You are as corrupt as the city itself, and you feast on its misery. So excuse me if I don't see a massive difference in your favor here."

I probably shouldn't have antagonized the hulking mass of a man like that. After all, the reputation I threw in his face was what had had me so scared of him in the first place, even if he did make my body ache and my pussy yearn. But after Lightning's betrayal—at least it felt like betrayal in the hollow part of my chest, regardless of how it really shouldn't —I'd had all I could take of overbearing superhumans who thought they could sweep into my life and mess me up with their stupid pheromones and archaic view of women.

"You of all people should know that things in this city aren't always what they seem," he replied, his voice irritatingly calm.

"Oh, so you don't murder people for sport?"

"No."

I arched both eyebrows in disbelief. "Yeah? Because

when I saw you use those swords, you looked pretty experienced in wielding them."

"I am. And I am very skilled at killing people, superhuman or otherwise. It is no secret that I have very little care for your human laws, but I do not murder innocents." He stroked a hand through a loose lock of my hair, seemingly contemplating the blonde strands. "And in concern to my claim on you...   I won't deny, I have possessive feelings toward you, my feisty little kitten. You are mine, and nothing you do will change that. I am sorry if that upsets you—not for claiming my right, but for any displeasure it may cause you. But if I ever hear you call yourself my whore again, there will be consequences. I do not need to brand my mark into a woman to get between her thighs. I *chose* you—and you accepted. The magic in that bond is much, much stronger than what your precious hero seems to believe."

I bit my lip and looked down from his calm, penetrating gaze in an attempt to get a hold of my swirling thoughts and emotions. I wanted to believe him when he said he didn't murder innocents, even if it was beyond stupid of me to trust the infamous villain's word.

And... I wanted to believe the warm pulsing from the nape of my neck that sent soothing tendrils through my body as he denied Lightning's claim to what the mark meant. I wanted it to mean more. It *needed* to mean more. The deep, confusing longing from the very marrow of my bones couldn't just be my body's reaction to their pheromones.

A gentle touch to my chin made me look back up. The Shade's eyes met mine, and I felt the pull from them like a near-physical force.

"I am here because I wanted to see you. Nothing more."

"It's the middle of the night," I said, dazed by the intensity in his gaze. "How did you know I wasn't asleep?"

"I didn't."

I frowned. "So, what? You were just going to watch me sleep? That's really fucking creepy."

His face lit up with a wry smirk. "What gave you the idea that I wasn't planning on waking you up? I believe I did warn you what would happen the next time you saw me."

Heat filled my cheeks at the memory of his parting words the last time he'd been in my apartment. "A light bit of night-time rape, then? That's not helping the whole creepy-thing, you know."

"Oh, Kathryn." The Shade leaned forward, pressing me backwards until my back hit the seat of the sofa with his mere presence. His eyes glowed with awakening heat. "If you keep calling it rape, I'll think you have a desire for power play. And I am very, very good at playing, my pretty kitten."

Oh. This talk had taken an entirely different turn, fast, and even though my body hummed with appreciation as the large male placed a hand on each side of my shoulders and hovered over me, I found it hard to just let go and forget about everything else that had happened in the past eight or so hours.

"And Lightning? I croaked. "It doesn't bother you that...?"

"That he fucked you?" The Shade scoffed. "His smell on you just makes me ache all the more to replace it with mine."

Nope, The Shade was apparently not the jealous type.

"Well, that and the mark-thing."

The Shade paused his slow prowling above me, his wide shoulders going rigid and his blue eyes darkening. "What *mark-thing?*"

"Uhm... he bit me again. I dunno, it seemed like marking?" I squirmed in my blanket-cocoon until I managed to twist my neck enough to expose the back of it.

The growl resonating from the large male on top of me made the first spike of fear hit my nervous system. I turned my head back around, and flinched at the absolutely murderous rage set in his clenched jaw, dark eyes and exposed teeth.

Or maybe he *was* the jealous type. *Crap.*

"The next time I see him, I'm going to fucking kill him!" he snarled. His hands gripped hard around the edges of my blankets, making the bulging muscles in his arms and chest flex in the process.

"Why is it so bad?" I squeaked, as my vocal cords were seemingly as tense as the rest of my body, trapped underneath his hulking form. "He marked me before you ever did."

"He half-marked you," The Shade growled. "*I* claimed you. *Me!*"

I wasn't about to discuss semantics with him, but it did seem like Lightning had managed to piss him off the same way he'd wanted to piss off Lightning—by placing a mark on top of his.

My contemplations came to an abrupt halt when the fury in The Shade's eyes shifted, and a heat I'd come to know all too well in the past few weeks flamed in its place.

With quick movements he ripped the blanket to pieces until I was lying naked in front of him, much like a kid would unwrap a Christmas present. He shed his gloves and then grabbed my breasts in both hands, holding them firmly enough that my nipples peaked at the light graze of his palms. Once they were hard and aching under his touch, he dipped his head and sucked first one and then the other into his hot mouth. I arched my back involuntarily as shivers crept from my aching points down my spine, until they reached my clit and made it throb with longing.

It was way too easy for him, as well as the man he'd sworn to murder for his trespassing, to turn me on. Shame at my wanton reaction to his advances made me put both hands on his shoulders and push. Hadn't I just spent a good hour sulking about being fucked and then dumped like yesterday's trash? Maybe happily writhing underneath whatever man happened to crawl through my window was what'd landed me in trouble in the first place.

"You need to stop that."

A low, disapproving growl was all the reaction I got. The Shade swirled his tongue around the nipple lodged in his mouth and sucked it deeply, making my hips rise of their own accord.

"I'm serious." I shoved harder at his shoulders. "I'm not some cum dumpster you can just roll up on whenever it suits you. I'm getting really tired of you two thinking I'm happy to spread my legs because of your pheromones and whatever claim you think you have on me. I don't like getting treated like a booty call for superhumans!"

The tongue playing with my nipple stilled. The Shade lifted his head off my breast slowly, until he was once again hovering over me, eyes locked on mine. Some of his previous anger flickered behind the heat.

"Is that why you've been crying? *He* made you feel these things?" His voice was dangerously quiet.

"No. Maybe. I just..." I let my hands flop back down on the couch, too overwhelmed with all the emotions running rampant in my head to even know what I was feeling.

Soft lips brushed against mine in a butterfly-light kiss. "I *will* kill him, both for the mark and for hurting your feelings. Will that make you happy?"

I blinked in shock. "No! No killing anyone!"

The Shade wrinkled his nose at my outburst, but didn't argue. Instead, he let a hand slip down between my thighs to caress my mound, teasing the slit with a gently probing finger.

"Will me pleasing your body without finding release myself make you happy, then?" The finger slid in between my lips and trailed up to tap against my clit.

I fought back a moan and arched an eyebrow at him. "I'm sorry, is the biggest, baddest villain in town offering to get me off without so much as a hand job in return?"

"Maybe the biggest, baddest villain in town isn't so bad after all?" he mumbled as he pushed his mouth to mine once more, this time kissing me more heatedly.

I was pretty sure he was, indeed, bad, despite something from the depths of my hormonal overload whispering about him being kinder and gentler than I'd ever imagined him capable of. What I wasn't sure about was why he spent so much time and energy trying to convince me he wasn't. It should be plenty obvious from our first encounter that I responded shamefully well to his dominance, so there really was no need for him to be so... gentle.

Unless he really did want to prove himself to me, for whatever reason I couldn't even begin to fathom.

I knew I should refuse him—I'd just slept with his arch-enemy, and no respectable woman offered herself up to a man like The Shade. But I didn't.

I'm not sure if it was curiosity, or the aching hollow still tearing at my chest after Lightning's dismissal that made me ask, "Will you stay with me after?"

The Shade hesitated for a moment, pausing his light teasing between my legs. I could practically see the wheels churn behind his hooded gaze as he weighed the risks.

Finally, he nodded once, and then reached out to fold me into his bulging arms before he stood up, carrying me bridal-style.

"Yes, kitten. I will stay."

EIGHT

I moaned as the fingers between my legs got more insistent in rubbing my tight clit, and instinctively spread my legs wider. The Shade dipped into my already soaking depths to lubricate his fingertips, and then returned to my nub. The smooth slide coaxed its hood back, and I jolted at the direct contact when his thumb and forefinger grabbed the exposed pearl. He was gentle, though, and expertly stroked me with short, precise caresses.

"There are so many things I could do to you, to make you writhe and beg," he whispered hoarsely against my neck. "I could tie you up and whip your delicious ass red and raw. Put clamps on your nipples and this pretty little clit. Make you take my fist. Why is it that all I want to do is be inside of you, rutting like a simple beast? What magic do you keep between these luscious thighs to make me crave nothing but your cunt's sweet embrace?"

Under normal circumstances, I would probably have taken his words as a threat. Now, though, when my head was swimming with the pleasure he rubbed into my clit and the teasing tickle of his featherlight kisses on my jaw, neck and shoulder, it only increased the heat in my abdomen threatening to boil over. My fluids seeped from my core, tattling on my body's easy surrender to any and all devious plans he might have for it.

The Shade slipped a finger not preoccupied on my clit down and pushed it inside my opening to the knuckle. I squeezed around him on instinct, and was rewarded when he curved his finger after my g-spot.

"Ah!" My hips bucked up at the delicious pressure and I grasped at the sheets until the teasing of my clit stopped.

Frustrated, I writhed and reached down to take over myself, but he caught my hand before it reached its goal.

"Bad kitten." His taunting voice wafted over my exposed pussy and lower abdomen, and then he pushed another two fingers into me. I gasped in pleasure at the stretch, and then again when his mouth descended on my still-throbbing clit.

This was so very different to the night in the alley. The Shade sucked and licked me almost too gently, while his fingers slowly moved in and out of my now soaking pussy. While he had been rough and dominant while having me up against the brick wall, he was now careful and tender... and the difference was driving me up the wall.

My need to orgasm increased with every flick of his tongue and every lazy circle against my frontal wall, but the stimulation was just light enough that I couldn't quite reach the point of no return.

"Please, Shade, more!" I moaned, trying to buck my hips up against his mouth for more pressure. He expertly followed my frantic movements, keeping the exact same contact as before. He didn't even bother to answer me, just hummed into my frantically clutching pussy and gave my quivering thighs a light squeeze.

"Please!" I grabbed for his head, forcing him down harder over my aching clit. Like a woman possessed, I ground myself against his lips and tongue, straining against the fire in my abdomen that burst forth now that I was finally getting the pressure I needed. I was so close, *so close!*

The Shade let me rub against him and calmly teased my g-spot until I was right on the edge, literally no more than a second from climaxing.

Then he sat up, easily slipping out of my frantic grasp.

"*No!*" The sharp burn of disappointment tore through my body. I slapped both palms against the mattress in frustration, not capable of restraining myself. "Fuck!"

His finger slipped back in place against my still-pulsing clit. He gently tapped it, shooting tendrils of excitement through my deflated body. "Patience is a virtue, little kitten. The longer I build you up, the more powerful the orgasm."

"Fuck that! Just... *fuck me!*"

It hadn't been my intention to ask for it, but the words blurted out of my mouth before I could even think about them. My entire body throbbed with the need to feel him in me—needed the hard stretch and roughness I knew he was capable of, and to hell with any delusions I had of virtue. All I needed was his cock inside of me so I could finally reach the peak my entire being was screaming for.

Something gleamed in his blue eyes, and when I saw his small smirk, I knew he'd played me to get exactly this result—me begging for his cock.

I didn't care.

"Now!"

"Anything you ask, lover." The Shade easily straightened

up on his knees and stripped out of the top half of his suit. I couldn't help my eyes from following the defined path of his muscles down to where his hands were opening his pants and sliding them down powerful thighs.

His cock sprung free, thick and heavy, and I bit my lip from voicing the sliver of concern the sight induced. He was roughly the same size as Lightning, and despite the intimidating view, I knew I could take him. My pussy clenched in agreement.

When he was completely naked, save the mask, he climbed back onto the bed and looked down on my naked and splayed body. The heat in his eyes washed over me, setting my already smoldering desire ablaze.

He fell on top of me, catching his weight in his hands, and I whimpered at the delicious press of his thick cock against my eager pussy.

At that point, it really didn't matter that I'd already been fucked by another that same night, and it didn't matter that the man between my widely parted legs was supposed to be the most dangerous man in the city. All that mattered was his strong body and its ability to sate all my desperate needs.

I wrapped my legs around his hamstrings and dug my fingers into his broad shoulders, mewling with need.

The Shade took it as the permission it was intended. He slid his hand over my left breast, squeezing it gently, before trailing down my stomach to slip between my folds.

I arched into him as he played with my clit. "Please, I need you inside of me!"

With a grunt, he grabbed his thick shaft and guided it to my entrance. I bit my lip at the near-painful strain as my pussy stretched to accommodate him, but thanks to my escapades in this very bed with Lightning only hours earlier,

I could take The Shade in one smooth push. My overworked muscles protested a little, but it only added to the thrill.

He bottomed out in me, and the ache in my chest brought on by the memory of the night with Lightning vanished in a rush of pleasure.

"Oh! Yes!"

His rich growl answered my call, the pleasure in its low rumble echoing my own.

"*More!*"

The Shade snapped his hips in response to my demand, forcing my pussy to cling to his girth as he pumped me just the way I needed.

I cried out, moaned, panted and whined underneath his body's forceful thrusts, lost in pleasure. My orgasm crashed over me after what felt like only moments trapped in this blissful state of rutting.

I screamed my pleasure out and dug my heels into The Shade's hamstrings in an involuntary attempt to still his movements while my pussy milked his length in euphoric spasms.

He drove into me a few more times, showing my body who was in charge, before he mercifully stilled and let me ebb from the powerful rush.

Once pleasant lethargy finally replaced the convulsions, I flopped down fully on my back, my arms and legs splaying open. "Wow. You superhumans really know how to fuck."

I don't know why I said that. The words just slipped out of my mouth as my blissed-out brain relished in the second dose of endorphins for the night, not caring one iota that the powerful male still buried in my pussy probably wouldn't appreciate the reference to my other lover's prowess.

The aggressive growl rumbling from The Shade's chest

confirmed as much. My eyes popped open in shock at the threatening sound, but before I could react to it, he'd pulled out of me and grabbed me by the hips, and suddenly I was face-down on the bed.

I squealed in surprise, and then grunted when he re-entered. Roughly. My used muscles protested, but The Shade's previous gentleness was gone, swept away by my reference to Lightning.

He drove in hard and set a punishing pace that had me clawing at the sheets every time he bottomed out. But I didn't object.

Not only did I have it coming, after my unfortunate slip —some sick and twisted part of my most primitive self also loved to be physically dominated and put in my place by a man strong enough to *make* me.

A tug on my hips pulled my ass in the air, but when I tried to raise up on my hands to ease the angle he was thrusting into me with, The Shade pushed me back down on the bed with a heavy hand on my neck.

I whimpered but didn't fight as he once again grabbed both my hips, giving me every inch he had in long, rapid thrusts.

I stayed on my knees with my ass thrust up and my pussy open wide to his continued assault until another orgasm began to build deep in my core.

As if he knew, The Shade pushed me down flat on my stomach and slid a hand underneath me to my clit, forcing sharp spikes of pleasure to mix with the deep sensations rolling through me from my battered channel.

Black dots danced before my eyes when I finally, mercifully, came.

My pussy clutched at the invading cock and I pressed

my hips down against The Shade's hand, rubbing my clit harder against his fingers until my violent climax eased its tight grasp.

I sagged against the bed, completely spent.

The Shade didn't move. He was still poised above me, one hand clutching my hip hard, the other trembling lightly against my now over-sensitive clit.

I groaned, knowing that he wasn't done and that I wouldn't get to relax in the afterglow just yet.

But he surprised me.

He found the strength to release my hip and clit, and though he remained within me, he didn't move. I could feel his cock pulse heavily inside my sore sheath and knew he had to be close to his own release, but he didn't take it. For whatever reason, The Shade kept his promise of not climaxing, even though he had manipulated me into begging for sex.

He rested on his fists above me while I slowly came down from my high. His labored breath swept over my neck and shoulders in harsh pants, and I could practically feel his urge to keep thrusting until he came. But he still didn't.

Instead, he bent his head to the back of my neck to nibble at my mark with his teeth. It was a bit harder than just a sensual, post-sex caress, but not hard enough to sting. The way he near-moaned when his teeth dug gently into my skin, I got the distinct impression it was only his iron will that kept him from re-marking me.

Eventually, he found the strength to roll off.

His still rock-hard cock slid from my sheath, and even in my thoroughly relaxed state, my walls clung to him as if begging him to stay. He flopped to his back with a suffering groan and pressed an arm over his eyes as if to block out the world.

A part of me wanted to release him of his promise. Another, undoubtedly meaner, part enjoyed his suffering just enough that I didn't. It felt good to be the one with the power, even if it was only mine because he'd given it to me. It was the first time with either superhuman I'd felt like my voice truly mattered, and I wasn't about to throw that away. Even if the thought of giving in made my pussy clench with longing.

"You okay?" I asked as I rolled over onto my side to look at him.

The Shade breathed deeply through his nose. "I'll be fine." Another deep breath, and then he removed his arm from his eyes and reached out for me, grabbing me around the waist and pulling me on top of his chest. His erection strained hard and demanding against me until I parted my legs and let it slip up between my thighs to rest against my puffy sex. He swallowed another groan at the contact, and I smirked against his skin.

Getting handled as easily as if I were a dainty little thing was starting to grow on me. It was completely impossible to feel too awkward, or too fat, when the man wrapping his arms around me was so strong that he could lift me without blinking, and so tall and coiled with muscle that I even looked tiny by comparison.

I propped myself up against his chest and looked down at his masked face. "You're staying?"

"I'm staying," he confirmed.

The low rumble of his voice against my chest felt good, soothing. I lay my head back down, just underneath his collar bone, and pressed an ear against his solid pecs. The steady thrum of his heart resonated deep inside of me, each beat of it calming my own. Even the heavy smell of sex and sweat in the air added to the tranquility.

Why did I find peace in the arms of someone I used to think was evil?

And when had I stopped thinking he was the worst villain in the city?

NINE

"Kathryn."

"Mm?" The deep voice only roused me halfway. I was so incredibly comfortable. I didn't want to leave my pleasant cocoon of sleep.

"Dawn is here. I need to leave now."

Leave? Reluctantly, I cracked open an eyelid. Pale light illuminated the loft, indicating that it was, indeed, dawn. A strong jaw and a black mask came into focus next, and I blinked in confusion when I realized that my comfortable bed was a man's bare chest.

Strong arms constricted around my torso, and I groaned I denial. I was *so comfortable.*

"Stay?" I begged sleepily, burrowing back down against the thick muscle underneath me.

He brushed a kiss against the top of my head. "I can't. I need to get back before the streets fill too much, or people will panic if they see my suit."

Panic? Suit? ... Wait, a black mask?

My eyes shot open when I remembered whose chest I

was sleeping on. The sudden shock of the morning light hurt, and I squinted up at The Shade.

He smiled softly and released my waist so he could brush away a lock of my hair that'd gotten stuck to the side of my face away. "I'll be back when I can. Sleep until you're rested, little kitten."

I automatically touched my fingers to my cheek where he'd brushed against me and found it wet. Splendid. I'd drooled in my sleep. A glance at his chest revealed that I'd also drooled *on* him.

Caught between confusion and embarrassment—a mix I was getting unpleasantly used to these days—I rolled off The Shade's chest and watched as he got out, stretched his bulging body so all the muscles on his back flexed intriguingly, and proceeded to get dressed.

I looked up at the man I'd spent the night with. Yeah, he was a bad man. He was dangerous, strong... and he had been inside of me, worshiping my body as if I was the most precious thing on the planet.

The Shade bent down and brushed his now gloved fingers over my sleep-swollen lips. "Until next time, my kitten."

I blamed the sleep-dampened rush of excitement at his words on my body, as well. There was no other reason for me to feel anything but dread at the prospect of seeing him again.

I DIDN'T WAKE up again until well past midday—a habit that seemed to come with too many run-ins with superhumans.

I stretched, my body protesting the move with a tenderness I'd recently learned was an inescapable side-effect of being well-fucked, and then spent the next twenty minutes sprawled out in bed, giving serious consideration to just staying there for the rest of the day.

When I finally did manage to pull on panties and a t-shirt, it was with the knowledge that I'd need to finish up my article to maximize the traffic. As much as my invitation to the event had been a ruse, I still needed the money it would bring in.

I spent the early afternoon finishing up little snippets of observation, complete with fawning over pretty dresses and famous faces, and uploading the appertaining pictures while drinking coffee, eating waffles, and doing my very best not to think about Lightning, nor The Shade.

Nothing good would come of dwelling too much on the night's events—nothing but a demanding throb from between my legs and a hollow feeling in my chest. I had absolutely no desire to work out what the latter part meant—not when Lightning had made it plenty clear that there was nothing between us apart from the mark, and The Shade... well, he was The Shade. Allowing myself to fall victim to his pheromones was one thing. Anything more... No. No, I was absolutely not going down that path.

I stared hard at my computer screen until my thoughts swerved back from the edge of insanity to once again focus on the picture of a smiling Leonora Ridgebane standing next to the mayor.

Life was a funny thing. A month ago, I would have been as excited about attending a party with the starlet and other members of the jet set. And now, when I'd actually been given the opportunity, I resented the hell out of it. Perhaps that came with having firsthand experience with how sick and corrupt it all was, and that the mayor and, undoubtedly, many others of the rich and influential people used their power against those of us in the less affluent section of the population.

It was with relief that I finally pressed "publish" on my blog post before I turned my attention to the other pictures on my phone—the ones I'd taken in the mayor's office.

I took a sip of my refilled coffee and unplugged my phone from the computer. After the near-miss with Lightning last night, I didn't want any trace of the pictures accidentally left behind anywhere once I'd deleted them off my phone.

It didn't take me very long to realize that bad guys don't keep entries conveniently labeled "Receipts of Evil Doing & Miscellaneous Underhanded Services" in their records, and that this whole venture would have been a lot easier if I knew exactly what I was looking for.

I stared intently at blueprint after blueprint of what looked like sewer systems and housing developments without seeing anything remotely interesting or suspicious. If there was some secret code hidden in these schematics, then clearly I wasn't bright enough to spot them.

After four cups of coffee, my eyes were starting to cross from looking so fixedly on my screen for what was nearing on six hours straight, and the many lines and curves looked more and more like the last set of lines and curves I'd searched through. Perhaps that's why I didn't notice anything amiss with the thirtysomething schematic I was perusing before I, by complete happenstance, glanced at the small print at the top right corner of the picture listing the name of the blueprint.

Blue Arrow.

I paused, finger poised over my screen to swipe left to the next image.

Aaron had said to look for a file named something along the lines "Blue Sparrow" or "Blue Jay." Blue Arrow was the closest thing I'd gotten.

I rubbed my eyes and looked at the schematics again, and frowned when the blurry lines sharpened for my tired gaze. What had looked like some high-tech thingamajig for a larger construction after page upon page of blueprints slowly took form into something... entirely different.

It took me a good few moments of staring at my phone before I realized what I was looking at.

A weapon. A large, scary-looking weapon.

I didn't fully understand the ins and outs of the little symbols scribbled along the margin, but even to my untrained eyes, it looked like a high-tech gun.

I put my phone down, chills suddenly making their way up my back and down my arms. Knowing the mayor was corrupt was one thing. It was another entirely to suddenly see hard evidence that he was involved in something this dark. Weapon development. *Christ!*

That's when I remembered the article by Peter Miller, which had resulted in his death. In it, he'd mention the mayor funding a weapon used by Bright during a bank robbery. Was this it?

And if so, were there any links in the financial records I'd pulled to show me where the money had come from?

Hastily, I flicked my screen to the pictures I'd taken of his "alternative budget." It only took me minutes to find an entry labeled "Blue Arrow." It showed several million dollars at the expense entry. Quickly, I wrote down the reference number listed next to the amount and began searching through the pictures I'd taken of the appendix linked to the alternative budget.

Fifteen minutes later I was staring at the name neatly lined up next to my scribbled down reference number.

Shaw Industries.

As in Elias Shaw, the billionaire who hid behind a mask when he saved me from the mayor's thugs, claimed me to protect me, and then took me so thoroughly I could still feel the ghost of his cock inside of me now.

The Shade had helped fund the mayor's horrific-looking weapon? Even if by some absurd twist of fate it wasn't the same weapon, why had The Shade funded it?

My stomach churned as bile rose in my throat.

He was as corrupt as his reputation predicted, completely unrepentant and evil to the core. Why he had lied to me about his involvement with the mayor, I couldn't fathom. To trick me into believing he wasn't evil? To get me to trust him, so I would surrender my body willingly?

My heart throbbed unevenly and unexpected tears blurred my vision. I was such a fool. Such a goddamn fool.

I breathed through my nose to try and calm myself down. It would do me absolutely no good to fall to pieces right now, and I needed to work out what I could do next. I had his mark on my neck, and after Lightning's comments last night, I couldn't exactly count on him to be the white knight who swept in to save me. I needed a plan to deal with The Shade, and I needed it now.

It took me a few moments, but slowly, my heart's rhythm began to even out again, and I could finally focus on suppressing the panicked swirl of thoughts and emotions.

There would be time to deal with my feelings of betrayal later.

I glanced down at my phone again, willing my brain into action. I couldn't confront The Shade with what I'd found. Partly because that would reveal that I knew his identity, and partly because I doubted he'd take kindly to being outed as working *with* the mayor, while pretending like he was trying to take him down. No, I couldn't—

An eerie tingle at the back of my neck, where my mark was located, made me pause mid-thought.

Someone was in my apartment. *Again.*

Panic bubbled up in my chest, completely overriding my sensible brain. I fumbled at my phone for what felt like an eternity before I managed to turn it off and slide it behind my computer, where it was hidden from view.

Okay, I could do this. I could face The Shade and pretend like everything was fine. If he wanted sex again, I could turn him down by saying I was too sore, or that I needed time to deal with everything from last night. Just a few sentences and he would be on his way.

"I know you're here," I called before turning toward the kitchen. "There's no need to lurk."

A beat's silence, and then...

"Well, then, I guess I better stop lurking."

The cold voice sent shocks down my spine, but it wasn't until he stepped forward from the shadows that my heart leapt into my throat with an entirely new sense of dread.

The masked man calmly striding across the floor toward me wasn't The Shade.

It was Bright.

My limbs felt leaden, as if they knew I could never outrun him, and trying would only make things worse.

I stared at the superhuman named after the bold, yellow streaks on his high-tech suit. He wasn't as infamous a villain as The Shade, but a high-profile robbery last December had put him squarely in the camp of *bad guys*. And here he was, in my apartment, looking at me with cold, glowing blue eyes.

I resisted the urge to check that my phone was properly hidden and kept my gaze on his masked face. He couldn't possibly know that I was on to whatever his connection was with the mayor. *Please, God, he can't know.*

"I hear you know an acquaintance of mine."

I blinked at the unexpected comment. "W-what?"

"There's a rumor swirling around certain circles that you and Lightning know each other rather *intimately*." He sent me a sickly smile. "Which your little demonstration before seems to prove. Did you expect him to come through your window, little mouse?"

I gaped at him for a moment, completely stunned. "I... what? Why do you care who Lightning sees? What do you want?"

His nostrils pulled up in disgust. "I hate humans who think they can talk to me like equals. I'll be asking the questions tonight, and you will answer. One way or the other."

I gulped when he touched a nasty-looking gun at his belt. "Got it?"

I nodded, holding both hands out in front of me in a useless attempt at shielding myself from the danger. But as I stared half-paralyzed up at the superhuman, I remembered that I did have a shield against harm from him and other supes.

With fingers shaking from relief I pushed my hair out of the way and turned my neck. "I've been marked! I am protected."

A look of surprise flickered behind the black and yellow mask before Bright dropped his gaze to my neck. A noise left his throat as he zeroed in on the place I'd been bitten.

In what seemed like one, smooth stride he was by my chair, a gloved hand closing around the back of my neck, just above the mark.

"So you have." His voice was cold and dangerous, and he increased the pressure on my neck until my spine objected. I bit down hard on my lip to not give him the satisfaction of hearing me whimper. "By nothing less than *two* supes. How curious. How very, *very* curious."

A pained groan escaped me when he yanked me up from the chair by my neck, seemingly not caring how much he was hurting me.

"I wonder if they care enough about you to explain to the Council how this oddity occurred. What do you think, little mouse? Do you think they'll come and claim you, for the world to see their shame? Two enemies, bound together by the same, worthless human girl! Somehow, I'm not so sure they'll be too eager to broadcast this. And if they don't show... well, I guess that means no one will mourn your death."

TEN

LIGHTNING

It was an unshakable itch, rooted somewhere in his chest and spreading through his entire body like a stubborn weed.

He'd tried to ignore it and had failed miserably. The first time he'd marked the human girl, constant, circling thoughts kept bringing his mind back to her, and he had more than once found himself halfway to her apartment before it dawned on him what he was doing.

It had been annoying as all fuck, but he had gotten through it without showing up on her doorstep and demanding she part her lush thighs for his cock. Doing his job with a constant erection had been very unpleasant, though. His suit just wasn't made to conceal a boner.

But now... Oh *fuck,* he was so fucking *screwed!*

He should have known better. He'd never taken things past a casual flirt with a girl while in his disguise before, and he should have stuck with that conviction. Even if seeing The Shade's mark on her creamy neck had unleashed a hurricane of hormones and possessive instincts like nothing he'd ever experienced before. Even if she was everything he yearned for... *Fuck!* There his rampant hormones went again! It was like being possessed by a very horny, very needy demon.

He should never, ever, have slept with her, because the onslaught of emotions that washed over him afterward had completely blindsided him.

Every instinct in his body was roaring for her, even after he'd sated his desperate desire inside her tight little cunt.

Nothing had ever terrified him quite so much.

There she lay, this fragile, soft little human, asleep in his arms and safe in the knowledge that he would protect her against all evil in this world. It wasn't the bone-deep understanding that he would give his life to protect her that terrified him, even if he didn't know why. It was the knowledge that she would count on him to keep her safe and protected at all times, and that he might fail.

There was so much evil in St. Anthony, so many people who could kill her in the blink of an eye, if he turned his back for even a second.

And if he failed her, and she died...

Lightning didn't understand the violent churn in his chest and gut at the thought of her death, but he vaguely recognized the feeling of terror mixed in with it.

She made him *afraid.*

In the middle of all the confusing emotions and raging instincts, he had resented her for turning him into someone who was scared.

He'd tried to snuff it out by making it perfectly clear to her that he had no intentions of any sort of romantic involvement with her.

The results had been... less than ideal.

Not only did it not make his newfound fear go away, it

added another, new concept to the exhausting range of emotions battering at him from the inside: guilt.

His dismissal had hurt her, and now he felt *guilt*.

It was infuriating.

Lightning rubbed a hand against the roof he was perched on, overlooking the ribbons of light moving with the traffic on the street below. Her roof.

He'd lasted, what, maybe eighteen hours?

Given how much his entire being *ached* for her, it was pretty damn impressive.

With a sigh he slipped out of his crouch and swung over the side of the building to enter her window. He had no idea what sort of explanation he would give her, but he'd think of something. Whatever mood she was in, he needed to be with her, and she would just have to deal with that.

Her apartment was dark and quiet when he slipped in through the window, and he frowned as cold tendrils of worry sprouted from the same place in his chest that housed the rest of the confusing emotions linked to the human girl he'd claimed.

She was probably just out for coffee, or meeting with a friend...

His heart spasmed unevenly at the thought of how he'd met her the first time—during a robbery at a coffee shop. Lightning pressed a fist to his chest, trying to force the unruly organ to relax.

This was getting ridiculous.

He wandered slowly out from the kitchen. At least he could spend the time until she came back looking through her things. Maybe even her bedside drawer.

Lightning smirked as he headed for the bed. She was so tight around him. Her pussy had clung to his shaft for each thrust. Whatever she kept in those drawers, maybe he should replace it with something bigger... call it mandatory exercise in between his visits.

His cock pulsed in agreement, but before he made it past her desk, his attention was caught by a small symbol carved into the wood.

The letter "B," surrounded by an angular design. Faint power shone from it, where the superhuman had infused it with enough of his essence to attract the eye of another supe.

Lightning's heart stilled in his chest while he stared at the symbol. It seemed to illuminate the empty apartment the longer he stared at it, emphasizing how lifeless and cold it was without Kathryn's warming presence.

A small note was neatly folded beside the carved letter. Lightning reached out and snatched it off the desk, unfolding it with one hand.

Shade, Lightning,

I will bring her to the council meeting on the 23rd.
If you want her back, come claim her. Together.

SHADES OF DARKNESS

DARKNESS III

Follow Kathryn's story in

Shades of Darkness

Pain. Violation. Degradation.

That's what getting involved with two magic-welding rivals has brought me. And the longer I stay with them, the deeper I'm sucked into the infested web of corruption running through every layer of my city.

I should try to escape—find a way out and away. No human can survive the demands of two such powerful men using her body as their battle ground.

But they are the only key I have to saving my city from the powers threatening to lay it to ruin.

And when the rest of the supe community learns of my existence, my two protectors have to decide what's more important: their age-old strife... or my life.

ALSO BY NORA ASH

THE OMEGA PROPHECY

Ragnarök Rising

Weaving Fate

Betraying Destiny

DEMON'S MARK

Branded

Demon's Mark

Prince of Demons

ALPHA TIES

Alpha

Feral

ANCIENT BLOOD

Origin

Wicked Soul

Debt of Bones*

DARKNESS

Into the Darkness

Hidden in Darkness

Shades of Darkness

Fires in the Darkness

MADE & BROKEN

Dangerous

Monster

Trouble